I0659387

DEAD RECKONING

A SINS OF THE MAFIA WORLD NOVEL

GWYN MCNAMEE

PROLOGUE

REAPER

The oppressive heat and humidity weigh down on my body like a heavy, wet blanket. Every breath draws hot, muggy air into my lungs, offering no relief. It's more like drinking in soup than breathing, really. Sitting in the thick, lush vegetation soaked with the recent rainfall doesn't help things, but it provides me the perfect vantage point to stalk my target. Complete cover where I can blend into the landscape and from which to deliver death.

He hasn't spotted me once since I began to follow him over a week ago, stalking him around town, assessing his every move, noting his patterns to find the perfect opportunity to strike. I could have killed him a thousand times, taken a shot that would end his life and make him pay for what he did to Evangeline. But I waited and bided my time for this exact moment. Because I knew that fucker was up to no good and that he wasn't up to it alone.

Nervous and excitable, the man practically screamed, "*Look at me! I'm doing it again,*" over the last few days. It matches the intel Cutter and Preacher provided me, suggesting he has repeated his new business venture since selling off his fiancée to human traffickers. He's found a new and easy way to make big money, and he's milking it for everything he can.

But waiting has paid off more than I ever could have hoped and opened the door for me not only to take out the fucker who betrayed Eva but also several of his contacts here in the islands responsible for the trafficking ring.

It's a win-win situation.

What more could I ask for?

This meeting place is ideal for what I have in mind to initiate his eternal punishment. The man doesn't deserve a quick death. Not when he put Eva and countless women since her through this kind of vile agony.

No, tonight he's going to pay for what he did in a way far more fitting.

First, I need to take out his buddies, the ones acquiring all the girls and selling them into their sinister version of Hell. I sight them all in my scope where they stand, talking near the rear of Danilo's car. One of them motions to the trunk and laughs.

Fuckers.

I have to bite back a growl because I know what's in the trunk. I know what my mark put there...or I should say *who* he put there. That poor girl he nabbed off the street only two hours ago before driving up here into the isolated hills to make the handoff to these assholes.

Confirmation that he's still up to his old tricks. The fact that the douchebag is still doing what he did to Elijah's girl makes this even easier. A true justification for what I'm about to do. Removing scum from the Earth has always been part of the job, but this one will taste especially sweet.

It's time for all these fuckers to meet the Grim Reaper.

I fire off five precise shots so fast the men don't even have time to react as their friends' heads explode and they crumble to the ground around each other. Danilo is the only one left standing, covered in the gore left by his soulless counterparts as they met their maker.

Surprise, you worthless piece of shit.

It takes him a moment to react. Long enough that I police my brass and am already on the move down the hill toward him before he finally manages to pull his phone from his pocket frantically. I reach into mine and press the button on the device that will jam the cell phone signals for miles around us.

He isn't getting help from anyone. Not up here. Not *ever*.

The man is so engrossed in trying to get his phone to work that he doesn't see me coming until it's too late. His head jerks up just as I reach him, and I grab him by the throat and pin him against the car.

His phone clatters to the ground as he scrambles and scratches at my arm, and I calmly lower my rifle to lean it against the car. His resistance doesn't faze me, barely even registers against the type of pain I'm used to enduring.

I meet his terrified brown gaze, his eyes free of any remorse for what he's done or empathy for the woman he has in this damn trunk. Only concern for himself fills them.

The desire to tighten my hold, to watch him gasp and claw at me while he struggles for a breath he'll never take again, surges through my veins. But that isn't the plan. I need him conscious enough to understand the message I'm about to deliver before taking his life.

I plaster on a wicked smile, the one I so enjoy using before I take the life of someone who doesn't deserve to have it. "Hello, Danilo. Eva sends her regards."

His eyes widen slightly, and he shakes his head, still clawing at my wrist, his nails digging at the flesh there.

I lean in to him and sneer. "There's no use fighting this. It's time for you to get what you deserve."

Truthfully, even this is too easy for a man like him—for *any* of these men. But I don't have the time to do what I really want, to break him down over days, tear him apart physically and mentally, draw out the death he knows is coming until he's literally begging for it.

So, this will have to do.

I grab my Yarborough knife from my boot with my free hand and drive it into his stomach in one smooth motion, then saw the blade back and forth as I pull it up and out, ensuring it does optimal internal damage and causes the most pain possible.

He opens his mouth to say something or to scream, but all that comes out is a strangled gasp and groan. I loosen my hold on his neck slightly, enough to allow him to take in a tiny breath.

"If-if you let me go, I'll tell you where you can find the others."

His words send ice shooting through my veins and goosebumps spreading across my skin despite the warmth of the night air.

The others?

Of course, there had to be more girls somewhere. An operation as big and well-put-together as the one that held Eva captive wasn't just some small upstart. It was established.

I've been hoping Danilo would lead me to any women being held here during the time I've been watching him, but it seems he's just a street supplier and not privy to any of the major workings of the organization behind this. So, I highly doubt he would have any useful information.

"Bullshit. You don't know anything."

He nods his head against my hold on his throat. "I-I do." He struggles to get the words out. "I heard them talking."

"Tell me." I shove my knife into his stomach again, ensuring the pain remains fresh and extreme as an incentive to be honest.

Another nod and gasp are all he can manage. "New York. Russians. Some club. I don't know the name."

"Russians?" I glance at the five dead men on the ground. "All your friends here are Filipino."

He gives a quick nod. "They-they're the suppliers. Get the girls onto the boats. But they work with these Russians from New York. And I also heard maybe some Albanians out of Chicago."

I growl and slam him against the car again, my anger flaring to life and heating the blood rushing in my ears.

These fuckers will create ties with anyone for a price, it seems.

That second part fits with what Cutter told me when he called to ask me for this favor. His crew had raided an Albanian boat on Lake Michigan filled with women who had been trafficked on their way to Chicago to be sold to the highest bidder. While Cutter assured me they took care of things on their end with the head of the family in Chicago to get things shut down there, this mission to locate Danilo and anyone on this side of the world who may have been involved fell to me.

But the Russian twist is unexpected.

It creates a new wrinkle in my plan. The mission was just supposed to be to take out this fucker, to make him *pay* for what he did to Evangeline, and maybe save a few more here in the process. But I can't stop knowing there are other innocent women out there, ones potentially being held and sold on US soil. Not when I can do something about it.

I jab my knife into him again, twisting and slicing, and he cries out, the sound echoing through the still night air. But out here, there isn't anyone to hear him. No one to hear the shots I took. No one to discover the massacre, perhaps for several days. Their choice of remote meeting spots sealed their fates tonight even though I've had them marked for death for far longer.

"You...said...you wouldn't kill me..." He barely manages to get the words out around the blood flowing out of his mouth.

I grin at him and stab again. "I said no such thing." Rage fills me as I spit in his face and watch it slide down over his blood-stained mouth. "You're getting what you deserve."

The second I release my hold on him, he crumples to the dirt, and I make my way to the trunk and pop it open. The girl lies bound and blindfolded, trembling, still in the school uniform she was wearing when I watched him lure her into his car back in the city before I followed him up here.

I reach out a hand to her arm, and she kicks out violently with her bound legs, some fight still in her despite what she's already been through at the hands of this monster.

"*Huwag kang magalala.*" My Tagalog is absolute shit, but I hope she understands what I'm trying to say to her, my assurance that she's okay and that I won't hurt her.

She freezes and turns her head toward me even though she can't see anything. Her bottom lip quivers, and tears slip from beneath the blindfold covering her eyes and down her cheeks.

I gently lay my hand on her arm. "Do you speak English?"

She offers a tiny nod.

"I'm gonna lift you out of the trunk and set you onto your feet. The men who took you can't hurt you anymore. You understand what I'm telling you?"

Even in the trunk, she must have heard the shots that took out Danilo's buddies, and she likely caught some of what I said to him, even if it was only muffled bits and pieces.

The girl is right to be scared of me.

She nods, trembling uncontrollably despite how suffocatingly hot it must have been in the trunk.

"Good." I reach in and scoop her up into my arms like she weighs nothing.

Her entire body vibrates so badly that when I set her onto her feet, I have to use my hand to steady her for a moment before she can get her balance. Using the same bloody knife that killed Danilo to cut the bindings at her ankles and wrists feels almost poetic, but when she reaches up to grab the blindfold, I capture her wrist with my free hand.

"Leave it on. Count to 200. Then get into this car and drive to the first police station you can find. You understand?"

She nods.

I can't take the risk of her seeing me and describing me to the police. I'd never get out of the country if they were looking for me. She seems to understand exactly what I'm saying without having to explain it further, though. Perhaps she can sense she's been saved and wants me to get away clean, even knowing what I just did.

This poor girl can't even comprehend what would have

happened to her had I not been watching and planning this already. If I had come next week, she'd be on a ship bound for only God knows where a day from now.

My heart tightens in my chest, and I release a deep sigh. I rest my hand on her shoulder, and she flinches. Rubbing gently, I lean into her. "You're going to be okay. I promise."

It isn't a promise I can make and definitely not one I can help keep in any way—that's one hundred percent on her and how she lets what happened affect her long-term—but I hope it's true. Like Eva, I pray she's able to move past what's been done to her and find a normal life with someone who loves her.

Not that we all get that. Some of us never will.

I glance at Danilo's cell. "There's a phone on the ground right near you. In case you need it. Tell them it belonged to the man who took you."

The man I came to the Philippines to kill lies bleeding out on the ground, gurgling and gasping for breath.

Mission accomplished.

He won't last long enough for any help to arrive, but it's still too good a death for him. It would have been nice to have a few days or even a week with him, to make him suffer and take him apart piece by piece. But I'll take this win, even if it isn't exactly how I wanted it.

Things rarely are. I've learned to accept that they never will be.

I give him one hard kick in the stomach. He cries out, and his former captive flinches and shifts away from the sound slightly but starts counting. "One. Two. Three. Four..."

Shit.

I never meant to scare her more, just needed to get in one last good one before I grab my gun and make my way back out across the small clearing to disappear into the darkness of the jungle.

It'll be like I was never here.

Get in. Get out. Nothing but bodies behind.

By the time she's done counting, the carnage will be the only evidence I was ever here.

A ghost.

A reaper on a mission to right this particular wrong.

It's the only thing I'm good at.

Except, it seems this is only the tip of the iceberg. Next stop—New York.

1

VIKTORIA

The deep bass thumps through the floor and straight into my temples, threatening to bring on a migraine I can't afford right now. I need to be one hundred percent on the ball tonight if I have any chance of catching something that might help the investigation. If what Hank said is true, breaking this case wide open will require absolute focus.

But just being in B66 makes unease coil around my spine and tighten with every passing minute. And it isn't just because Hank asked me to come here with him during off-duty hours, without a formal open investigation, on what appears to be some sort of shady tip he received from some "mystery" source.

I'm all for using who I need to on the streets to gather intel, but infiltrating a club owned by the Russian Bratva carries a risk far higher than anything else I've been involved with since becoming one of NYPD's finest.

I joined the force so I wouldn't end up in a place like this

—like so many of the girls I grew up with who had big dreams but ended up slinging drinks and sucking dicks just to make ends meet month to month, or feel like they belonged somewhere.

This club is a magnet for desperate women like them and men with too much money and lacking any morals. No wonder Hank suspects it's the center of the human trafficking ring we've long known runs here in NYC.

So, while I may have fought hard to stay away from places like B66, knowing what might be happening here to innocent women means taking one for the team and coming to see what I can spot, regardless of how uncomfortable it may make me.

Though, truth be told, maybe it's more than this space and the people in it making me uncomfortable. Like the man at the end of the bar across from us.

Tall.

Muscular.

Dark.

And despite there being any number of threats in the club—gangsters carrying unregistered, loaded weapons, women selling themselves, and drugs, the potential for a familiar face—I can't seem to drag my attention away from *him*.

He's new—if he were a player in town, I would recognize him. He has one of those faces you can't forget—strong, stubbled jaw, piercing blue eyes visible even from this far away—and despite my best efforts to keep my focus where it needs to be tonight, something about him keeps drawing my attention that way.

And it isn't just how handsome he is.

Something's off about him, and it has been since the minute he walked in here and took a seat on the stool.

His gaze never stops moving—from the door to the patrons, up to the balcony from where Yankovich runs his empire. He scans the club like he's looking for someone or waiting for something to happen. Dozens of scantily clad women work the floor and try to sidle up next to him, offering everything from drugs and drinks to sex, but the guy doesn't seem interested in the slightest. He offers them a little half-smile that doesn't reach his eyes and says something that has them scurrying away quickly. Yet he remains almost completely still, calm and casual—at least, to the untrained eye. But to me, it's clear—he's here for something else.

Maybe the same thing we are.

The rumor is they're still trafficking women brought in from all parts of the world. Innocents snatched off the streets and even straight from their homes, then thrown on huge cargo vessels to live in squalor for weeks or even months, making their way across to the States where they're sold into sexual slavery to the highest sick bidder.

I nudge Hank with my elbow and incline my head toward the mystery man while making it look like I'm just leaning in to talk over the loud music. "The guy at the end of the bar."

Hank raises an eyebrow and surreptitiously glances at him over his shoulder while he takes a sip of his beer. "What about him?"

"I think he's here looking to buy." And I don't mean drugs.

"What makes you say that?"

I continue to keep my eye on the man while pretending to laugh at something Hank said. It's important we blend in here. If we get made as cops, this could end with a lot of bloodshed. And while I wouldn't mind seeing some of

Yankovich's men in body bags for what they've done, I prefer to keep Hank and myself out of them. "Watch the way he's looking around. He isn't paying any attention to the girls on the floor. He's searching for something or someone in particular."

"Yankovich?"

"Maybe?"

It would make sense if he's here for the same reason we are. Yankovich runs this place and the bratva in NYC. He's the one who will be in charge of any trafficking that's happening. The man who will need to approve all buyers.

"I haven't seen him come down from the second floor once since we got here, though."

Nor would he.

Yankovich is smart enough not to get his hands dirty, especially somewhere as public as this. Anyone could walk in off the streets and witness deals handled up on that balcony. He won't want to be seen doing anything that could get him put away.

I fucking hate smart criminals.

They're the hardest to catch and usually the ones getting away with the nastiest stuff. The kind of stuff that keeps people like me—who have to clean up after it and deal with the aftermath—awake at night.

Hank wraps his arm around me and leans in close, both of us trying to make it appear like we're here as a couple and so we can ensure our conversation isn't heard by any curious ears near us. Though, with as loud as it is in here, that's unlikely, anyway. Perhaps the *one* positive note to the noise pounding on my brain relentlessly. "What you want to do? Want to grab him?"

I place my hand over his on my shoulder and brush my mouth against his ear while peeking at the man out of the corner of my eye. He hasn't moved from his perch at the bar, and his disinterested demeanor hasn't changed, either. "Watch him. See if we can get any confirmation of what he's doing here."

There isn't much else we can do at the moment. We haven't witnessed anything illegal yet, other than girls disappearing down the back hallway with bar patrons. But what happens behind the closed doors back there is the least of our worries. The girls on the floor here are doing it willingly and aren't our primary concern. While I'd love to get them out of this life, help them clean up and get decent jobs that don't require them to spread their legs or gag on cock for money, it's the women who don't choose it and are bought and sold who are our focus tonight.

A nod of his head confirms Hank agrees with the plan to wait and watch. So, we pretend to flirt and slowly sip at our drinks while maintaining a close watch on the man and the rest of the patrons in case anyone else interesting shows up.

With Michail Yankovich safely tucked up in the private balcony on the second floor, overseeing his kingdom but keeping his distance from the action, it won't be easy to nail him on anything. But if we can get an insider, someone who will feed us information, or someone we can put the screws to for cooperation, we just might be able to bring down the man responsible for so much misery.

Maybe it's wishful thinking on my part, but I have to believe good will triumph over evil, or I couldn't do this job day in and day out. Seeing what we do every day, the destruction and vileness humans show to each other, weighs on my soul in a way I never imagined it could. It's the only reason I agreed to Hank's off-the-books trip here tonight in the first place, but now that I'm here, I can't just walk away without *something* to show for it.

And that moment might have finally just come...

"Hold on." I tighten my hand on Hank. "Alexei Kosofik just came out of the back hallway, and the guy grabbed him."

Hank chuckles. "He has some balls to lay his hands on Kosofik."

"Or he's really stupid."

Something tells me that's not the case, though. This guy is too careful. Too meticulous in how he's leaning against the bar, how he's watching everyone, how he moves and doesn't put his back to the front door.

Something is definitely off here.

REAPER

I sip at my tonic with lime and scan the bar for what feels like the hundredth time since I arrived. Definitely isn't the type of place I want to be spending my evening and hanging out. But when I got to New York and started talking to the people in the know, all streets led me here. And to Michail Yankovich.

"They can get you anything you want. Their auctions are the best I've ever been to."

I cringed having to hear the way the people I pretended to befriend talked about these women...children even. Like they're a commodity to buy and sell and broker to the highest bidder rather than human beings with families and lives and hopes and dreams that were destroyed when they were taken. But I can play the part. I can play *any* part to get to my end goal. So, I smiled and nodded and said the words

I needed to get me here—to B66, the center of the bratva's activities in the city.

Now all I need to do is find Alexei Kosofik, Yankovich's underboss. The bastard hasn't shown his face here the last three days I've been hanging around, and the rumor mill suggests another auction will be happening soon. That means I don't have a lot of time to fuck around. He's likely busy making final preparations, but if I want to get to the girls before they're sold out from under my nose, I need to *find* them first. That will only happen through *him.*

I turn and lean back against the bar so I can appear to casually glance up at the private loft where Michail Yankovich always stays—just out of reach of anyone except those he deems worthy. I haven't seen him set foot down here once, even though this is his place. The man uses his balcony like a throne to lord over his kingdom, not caring about the fact that what he's doing to these women is destroying not just their lives.

He doesn't pay any attention to me watching him from below, just scans the crowd, then returns to the leather couch against the wall to drink and chuckle with his cronies.

Fucking asshole.

Men like him are the reason I joined the military in the first place, only I never expected to find them on US soil. At least now that I've been forced into retirement, I can stay busy using the skills good ole Uncle Sam gave me to eliminate fuckers like him and ensure innocents aren't caught up in his enterprise of filth.

I turn back to the bar and take another sip of my drink while I survey the club. The brunette across the bar, who I've caught watching me a few times, locks green eyes with me for a second before she darts her gaze away with a sweep of her long, dark hair and leans in to murmur something to the man next to her.

He wraps his arm around her as if they're a couple and he's drawing her closer, but the body language is all wrong. I snort and crunch on a piece of ice. They're clearly cops. It couldn't be any more obvious if they had a neon sign above them pointing down that read, "*The Fuzz.*"

And likely, they're here for the same reason I am— because the Russians are up to no good. The girls are just one very small portion of their business, but it's a lucrative one. One I intend to use to get my foot in the door and the information I need.

Speaking of doors...

The one that leads down the back hallway opens. Private rooms lie beyond it, and I keep seeing the dancers and waitresses disappearing down there with customers. Alexei Kosofik steps out, adjusting his cock behind his zipper.

This might be my only chance.

Before he can make it too far past me, I reach out a hand and grab his arm, stopping him in his tracks.

A stupid move for anyone, but intentionally so on my part.

It has to appear that I'm an idiot who doesn't know what he's doing. Some Midwestern farm boy who made his way here to purchase something very specific but who is naïve and clueless about the ways of this very dark world.

I plaster on my most idiotic smile. "Hey, are you Alexei Kosofik?"

He shoves off my hand and steps in to me with a snarl, puffing out his chest. "Who the fuck is asking?"

I retreat a bit, shrinking back and holding up my hands in surrender, trying to appear intimidated by his display even though I could kill him with my bare hands in ten seconds right where we stand. "Got your name from an old friend. He said you might have what I'm looking for. Potentially in red?"

Kosofik eyes me for a moment, from my dirty boots, up over my jeans and black T-shirt. "Who is this old friend of yours?"

I shrug and glance around but don't see anyone paying us much attention aside from the brunette. "He asked that I not use his name. You know, given the circumstances. But I have money. Whatever it takes to find what I'm looking for. It's hard to come by where I'm from."

He makes a scan of the club, then inclines his head to the bartender, who hands him a leather-bound menu. Holding it up, he leans into me. "You tell me what you're looking for, then you give me your cell phone number and I'll text you with the time and location."

Progress!

I smile at him and grab the "menu" from his hand. Acid climbs up my throat as I flip it open and read the pages. Of course, they aren't stupid enough to make what they're selling obvious. It's disguised as a "wine" list, with characteristics of the girls described in terms that any layperson would never think suspicious.

Red blend – 2014 vintage. South American grown fruit.

The lime tonic water churns violently in my stomach.

A fucking seven-year-old child.

I have to force myself to stay unaffected and close the menu slowly. Handing it back to Kosofik, I smile. "The red blend from 2000, Romania, would be lovely."

He nods and grabs a napkin and pen from the bar, and I hastily scribble down the number for the burner phone I bought.

"What's your name?" The question holds every ounce of

suspicion he still has about me, so it's time to really turn on my act.

"Adam Jones. From Minneapolis." The lie rolls off my tongue easily. And I know enough about Adam's life before he died to answer any questions this guy might have when he undoubtedly checks up on me before sending me any further information.

I'm sure Adam wouldn't mind my using his identity for this good cause. He died protecting the innocent, and now, his name can help save others.

Rest easy, brother.

Kosofik nods toward the front door. "I suggest you leave now."

I hold up my hands and back away. "I'll wait for your text."

He scowls and watches me leave. Giving him my back feels wrong and foreign and goes against everything I've ever been trained to do when it comes to the enemy, but it's a necessary action here. He has to believe I'm too stupid to do anything to interfere with their operations—just some farm boy completely out of his element in the big city looking for something only they can supply.

The second I step out the door into the not-so-fresh city night air, I light a cigarette and make my way toward where I parked the rental truck down the street. Footsteps follow behind me—light and casual. Someone who knows what they're doing and likely wouldn't be noticed by anyone else.

As I near the end of the building where the alley starts, the man with the brunette darts around me and steps out to block my path. The footsteps behind me stop, and I glance over my shoulder to find her only a few feet back, at the ready should I make any attempt to flee.

I take a drag off my cigarette and twist back to raise an

eyebrow at the man in front of me. "Can I help you with something, officer?"

He scowls at me and glances toward the front door of the club, probably concerned someone heard what I just said, but we're too far from it for anyone to have been alerted to who and what he is—that is, if they didn't already know given how obvious it was to me in the club.

I drop my cigarette to the sidewalk and grind it out with my boot.

His gaze follows the movement, and he raises an eyebrow at me and inclines his head toward the woman behind me. "Cuff him."

Shit. I do not *have time for this.*

I sigh and roll my eyes. "What's the charge, officer?"

The cop sneers at me as his partner grabs my wrist and jerks it behind me. My first instinct is to knock her back, take them both out, and hightail it out of here before they know what hit them, but that would only put a target on my back from the NYPD. That's the last thing I need when I'm on a mission like this.

He steps forward and reaches down for the cigarette butt on the sidewalk. "Littering. In violation of New York City Administrative Code Section 16-118."

Smug fucker.

I smirk at him as his partner secures the cuffs to my other wrist.

This is annoying and will eat up valuable time when I could be gathering more information and preparing for what I'm going to need to do, but at least it will be entertaining to fuck with New York's finest.

2

VIKTORIA

"Something is so off about this guy." I stare at the screen showing the video feed from inside the interrogation room where we're holding the man we grabbed from B66.

Roderick Dixon—at least according to his ID.

Hank glances up at me from his phone, which he's been glued to since the moment we got back. "Why do you say that?"

I sigh and slouch down into my chair. "We've been letting him stew in there for two hours and he's barely moved. He's just sitting there, like a damn statue. Most people would be restless, sweating, nervous. But not this guy."

"So, what are you thinking?"

I sigh and push to my feet. "I don't know yet, but I'm going to find out what the hell he was doing at B66."

Hank shifts uneasily and peeks at his phone again. "I,

uh, need to go make a phone call. You start with him. You're always good at getting under the skin of these types."

Making a phone call instead of interrogating our potential way into B66? What the hell are you up to, Hank?

I narrow my eyes on him. It doesn't make any sense for him not to want in on this questioning. The whole stakeout was his idea in the first place, his deal. Something is going on with my partner, too, but I can only handle one man at a time. And right now, the one in that room has to take priority. I can deal with Hank and make him fess up later. "Make your call quick."

He inclines his head in acknowledgment before I head down the hall to the interrogation room. Whatever Mr. Dixon's deal is, he's going to come clean to me tonight. It's too important for him not to. If what Hank suspects is right, there are innocent girls out there who need to be found —fast.

Even when I unlock the door and push it open, Dixon doesn't flinch. Doesn't even look my way, just stares straight ahead like he's sleeping with his eyes open. For all he seems to care, he could be sitting on a beach, relaxing under the sun instead of stuffed in here, with no windows, very little airflow, on a rickety chair.

The door closes behind me with a click, and I slowly lower myself into the chair across from him. Blue eyes meet mine, but they give away nothing. Perfect glassy pools I could swim in—but blank.

How the fuck does he do that?

I shove his pack of Marlboros and his Zippo across the table to him. "Thought you might want one of these. You've been in here quite a while."

He smirks at me, the first sign of any emotion I've seen from him since we grabbed him outside B66, and reaches out to take what I've proffered. Large hands deftly light a cigarette, and my focus follows as he brings it to his mouth and takes a drag from it with his perfect lips.

Shit. I'm staring.

It's hard not to with a guy like this. There's just something about him. The way he carries himself. The way he speaks. He's the kind of man who could be lethal to a woman's libido, and likely in other ways, too.

I force myself to meet his eyes, and he raises a brow at me, waiting for me to speak. "What were you doing at B66, Mr. Dixon?"

Dixon releases a plume of smoke into the air and leans back in his chair casually, crossing one arm over his barrel chest, causing his dark T-shirt to pull tightly across his well-formed pecs and biceps. "I thought you arrested me for littering."

Smartass.

"We did, and you'll be charged with that, but it doesn't mean we can't chat about something else."

He offers me a casual shrug that I know is anything but. It's all an act, one he does well. "I was there for a drink."

Lie.

"No, you weren't. The bartender poured you tonic and lime—all night. He never put a drop of alcohol in anything that you drank."

A grin he fights tugs at the corners of his lips, and he takes another drag, releasing a smoke ring that slowly dissipates in the air between us. "You were paying attention. I'm impressed."

I snort and shake my head, fisting my hands on the top of the metal table. "Why is that so shocking? A woman can't be a good, observant cop?"

His brow furrows, and he shifts forward slightly to tap

his cigarette into the ratty-looking ashtray on the table. "No. Because I figured you had more important things to worry about than what I was drinking, like Yankovich."

Yankovich.

My heart thunders against my rib cage. I certainly hadn't expected him to bring up the man we were there for, but it gives me the opening I'm looking for. "What do you know about him?"

Dixon shrugs again and takes another drag, blowing the smoke out the side of his mouth. "Just that he owns the place."

Bullshit.

A man like Dixon doesn't just hang out at a place like B66 for shits and giggles, ignoring the girls and *not* drinking. And I don't like dancing around the truth, let alone being *lied* to. "What was in the leather menu Alexei Kosofik handed you?"

The blue of his eyes darkens slightly as he leans toward me and snuffs out the cigarette in the ashtray. "A drink menu. So I could order something a little more interesting than tonic water."

Fucking smartass. This isn't going anywhere.

I scowl at him, shove away from the table, unlock the door, and storm out of it, letting it click closed behind me, locking him in. We've barely gotten started and he's already rattled me. Instead of me getting under *his* skin, he's managed to worm his way under *mine*. And I can't lose my cool in there with him. That would get us nowhere fast— even more *nowhere* than we already are, that is. I need to figure out who and what this guy really is so I can come back better prepared and break down that wall of smug machismo he exudes.

Entering the squad room, I spot Hank down the hallway

toward the bathrooms on his phone and motion him over to our desks.

He ends his call and approaches me, eyebrows raised. "Well?"

I drop into my chair and slam my fist on the desk. "Nothing. But he definitely knows something."

Hank grabs a single sheet of paper off my desk that I hadn't even noticed. "Not much on his criminal history check."

I grab the sheet that must have been dropped off after I went into the interrogation room and scan it quickly.

Nothing. Literally nothing.

There isn't a single speeding ticket, arrest, not even a damn *parking* ticket listed on this guy.

"*This* is all we have on him?"

No one is a ghost. No one. Everyone has a past. Everyone has skeletons hiding in their closets—even me. And with the way Hank is acting, it sure seems like he might, as well. All I need to do is find Dixon's and I'll have a way to get him to talk.

Hank shrugs. "Apparently so."

"Impossible...unless..."

Unless someone cleaned *up anything so no one would ever find anything.*

"What are you thinking, Vik?"

"Special ops, maybe?" I fire up my computer and grab the phone off my desk to call in a favor. "I'm going to see what I can dig up on this guy."

"Do you want to cut him loose?"

"No. Give me some time to see what I can find."

Hank motions toward the interrogation room. "Let me go see if I have any better luck with him in the meantime. We can play bad cop/good cop."

I snort and shake my head. "Which one am I?"

Hank smirks at me and shrugs. "Remains to be seen."

He makes his way toward the interrogation room as I dial a number I know by heart. I don't like asking for favors when it can get someone in trouble, especially the *illegal* kind, but there's only one person I know who has access to military records.

Anya answers on the second ring. "Vik? What's up?"

I glance around the room to ensure no one is within earshot. It would be very bad if anyone overheard the request I'm about to make. "I need info on someone I think is special forces, may be active, potentially retired."

She sighs. "And I suppose you don't want me to tell you how I get it?"

"Exactly."

Using Anya to get information that would otherwise be unavailable isn't at the top of my list of favorite things to do. I've only asked for her help once before, and it's weighed on my conscience ever since. I'm a good cop who likes to do things by the book, but special times call for special measures, and something tells me Roderick Dixon won't be easy to nail down—at least, not by any legal means.

"Give me what you have, sis, and I'll see what I can do."

REAPER

I take a drag off my cigarette and fiddle with my lighter—flicking it open and closed, the click of the lid the only sound in the room while I wait...again. The familiar feel of the metal in my hand threatens to bring up memories I can't possibly deal with right now.

It would be dangerous to let them come to the surface while I'm in a place like this and need to maintain my cool. Despite their best efforts to get me off my game and rattle me, it won't happen.

This is too important to fuck it up. The memories of how I got this lighter and what it's been through with me will remain buried under years of scar tissue intended to keep them at bay for as long as is humanly possible.

Hopefully, forever.

I wouldn't be surprised if they left me in here that long. They likely would if they legally could. Those two seem the type to think letting me stew will get me to break. That thought brings a smile to my lips as I take another pull off my cigarette. So does remembering the flash of anger in the brunette's eyes when I refused to give her what she wanted. That woman's passion simmers barely beneath her restrained surface, ready to burst.

The doorknob turns, only instead of the sexy brunette entering, it's her partner who walks in with a sneer on his lips. He smooths a hand over his beard, meeting my gaze with a hard one of his own.

Well, this is a surprise. I thought she would come back for round two.

I raise an eyebrow and lean back in my chair. "Your turn?" I cross my arms over my chest. "You two really got a thing for littering, huh?"

He pulls out the chair across from me that his partner occupied less than an hour ago and slowly lowers himself into it. This would be much more enjoyable with the pretty brunette, but it seems they've decided to play good cop/bad cop with me.

Though, I'm not entirely sure which one is supposed to be which.

His sexy partner was definitely annoyed and flustered during our brief conversation, but she wasn't hostile or aggressive. More like hot and bothered—though maybe that was just me bantering with her. Our interaction definitely did *good* things to my body.

I guess that means this man is the "bad cop."

He leans back in his chair, crossing his arms over his chest, matching my position. It's probably meant to be intimidating, but this guy is anything but. Cops don't scare me. Not much does anymore after everything I've seen and done. After that much blood, that much violence. The violent nature of the human race. What madmen will do for power. I thought nothing *could* affect me anymore.

Until now...

The thought of those girls getting sold off to sick fucks who will use them for all sorts of depraved torture brings up a fear I've never experienced. That poor girl from Danilo's trunk back outside Manila. The way she shook uncontrollably. Her flinching away from my touch even when it was meant to help and comfort her. It got to me, more than I'd ever admit out loud to anyone.

"Cut the shit, Dixon, or whatever the fuck your name is. The only hang-up my partner and I have is that we're both desperate to keep the streets of New York clean, and I'm not referring to your fucking cigarette, but I think you already know that."

Of course, I do.

They wouldn't have been at B66 if they didn't already suspect something shady was going on there; though, what they actually know remains to be seen. My information about the ring came straight from the source—Danilo pointed me in this direction before I left him to die, and there isn't any question he was involved with it since Evangeline made it clear who sold her. Then my people here only confirmed what I already knew.

What these cops know is another story. I'm sure they have their own sources, people they may trust, but that doesn't mean *I* trust them or the information they might have.

Detective Grayson uncrosses his arms and leans forward, propping his forearms on top of the metal table. "I think you and I aren't all that different. Hell, I think we were both at B66 for the same reason."

I quirk an eyebrow. "You looking for a piece of ass, too?" I angle my head and tip my chin toward the door. "If that's the case, the next time, you might want to leave the arm candy at home."

There was no way he was going to get anywhere with Yankovich or Kosofik with a woman like his partner hanging all over him. The men they *want* at their auctions, buying their women, aren't going to show up with one as poised and beautiful as Detective Garin to make a fucking purchase.

He clenches his fists on the table and nods, the evidence of his annoyance and frustration building just like it did with his partner when she was in here.

I bet he doesn't even know I can tell he's biting the inside of his cheek.

"That's good advice, and I might buy that you were in there looking to get laid if you had paid an iota of attention to the bitches hanging on your arm, but you dismissed every one of them. I saw the exchange with Kosofik."

I raise an eyebrow at him again. "And?"

I'm not about to offer him the information he's so obviously fishing for. He doesn't know jack shit and has nothing on me to keep me here once they issue the "littering" charges that I can no doubt easily have dismissed after paying a simple fine.

"*And* you're wasting your fucking time. My father wrote the book on vigilante justice, man. He helped take down Yankovich's two brothers, but it took him years to do it. You're in over your head, and I don't have time to waste on you, so you have a choice to make. Either you stand the fuck down and drop whatever it is you're doing, or you tell me what you know, and we nail this guy to the cross before any other girls go missing or get hurt."

Stand the fuck down? Who the fuck does this guy think he is?

There's no way I'm letting him or his partner get in the way of my mission. We may have a shared goal, but I made a promise to Cutter that I would make Danilo and everyone else responsible pay for what they did to Eva. Cutter came to me for a reason—he knows I won't stop until every single one of them who had a hand in it is six feet under.

Cops only fuck things up. Their hands are tied by rules and regulations. Worries about superiors and the law. Nothing will hold me back when the time comes, and I can't have them fucking things up with their ethical bullshit.

Detective Grayson pushes back his chair and stands. "I can't keep you here. But I can promise you that if you get in my way, there is an army of people who have no fucking problem making you disappear."

I snort and chuckle. "I'd like to see you fucking try."

This guy has no idea who he's dealing with. But if he interferes with my mission again, he's soon going to learn what I'm truly capable of.

He reaches into his jacket, pulls out a business card, and lays it on the table. "If you want this guy so badly, you're going to have to go through me." He nudges the card toward me. "Choose wisely, Dixon."

The door shuts behind him, and I reach out and grab the card, turning it slowly in my hand.

Choose wisely.

It sounds like something Dad would have said to me before I left the house on a Friday night as a teenager. But it's clear, it wasn't just a warning. It was a threat.

Detective Grayson may have more balls than I thought.

If he has even an inkling of who I am, threatening me takes on a whole different meaning. He's putting a target on his back, one I can easily hit...even with my fucking eyes closed.

Game on.

3

VIKTORIA

I lean back in my chair at my desk and release a heavy sigh into the phone, staring at the stain on the old, warped ceiling tiles I've watched slowly grow over the years. "Thanks, Danny. I appreciate you trying."

"Sorry I wasn't much help, Vik."

"Not your fault. I'll talk to you later." I end the call and toss my phone onto my desk a little too hard, sending it skittering across the marred wooden top.

Another dead end.

I don't know why I thought my friend over at the FBI might be able to find something I couldn't on Dixon, but I had to pursue every avenue available while I wait for Anya to work a miracle. Then again, if my suspicions about him are right, then maybe Danny *did* find something and just can't or won't tell me. Government secrecy and all that shit. Either way, my frustration has built enough to start a throbbing in my temples.

Maybe Hank is having more luck with him.

It might be our only hope of finding out what his interest is in Yankovich and B66.

I push away from my desk to check on the interrogation, but my ringing phone makes me turn back. Anya's name flashes across the screen.

Please have something...

Dropping back into my chair, I grab my phone and answer, "Hey, did you get anything?"

"You were right."

I grin and lean back, rubbing at my temple with my free hand. "I typically am, but what about this time?"

Anya snorts. "This guy you asked me to look into. I assume you don't want to know how I got the information."

Guilt churns the acid in my stomach. "I don't." I drop my hand and glance around the squad room to make sure no one is within earshot. "What did you find?"

"He joined the army at eighteen, right out of high school, and by the time he was twenty-two, he had been moved to the Combat Applications Group at Fort Bragg."

"Combat Applications Group? I don't get it."

"That's one of the code names for Delta Force."

"Shit. So, I was right?" It certainly explains a lot.

"Yeah, so it looks like he was a member of that unit for the last ten years or so. Retired about six months ago."

"He seems pretty young to retire."

The sound of her clicking on a keyboard floats through the line. "Looks like a medical discharge. I haven't been able to get into any more specific files because those things are locked up tighter than Fort Knox, but it's possible he was injured."

"He sure looked healthy and fit to me..." The way his hard muscles flexed under his T-shirt with every little move he made at the club and in the interrogation room definitely suggests a man in good shape.

But what the hell is a former Delta Force operative doing at B66 and getting tied up with Yankovich?

"Were you able to get anything else?"

Anya scoffs. "Do you have any idea how difficult *that* was to get? How about a thank you?"

I rub my eyes, trying to combat the growing migraine building behind them that seems to have migrated from my temples. "You're right. I'm sorry. Thank you. But did you get anything else? Anything I might be able to use? Maybe where he came to New York from or something that might be able to get him to realize he needs to talk?"

"Vik, this guy likely has resources you can't even imagine. Even retired, he has a skill set and training that make him more than capable of handling an interrogation from a New York City cop. And he likely has access to all sorts of different identifications, passports, and travel documents. Even if I tried to track him or where he's been, there is no way to know what name he was traveling under."

"Shit." I slam a palm against my desk and get a few looks from some people in the squad room. "I hadn't even thought about that."

"Who is this guy? Why are you so interested in him? Is he a suspect?"

Is he?

He was definitely acting suspicious at B66, and his little talk with Kosofik suggests he may be looking for the girls. But *why* is less clear. He doesn't strike me as a buyer, but that doesn't mean he isn't working for someone who is—perhaps picking up the "package" and delivering it to the sick fucker making the purchase.

"I can't tell you. Even if I wanted to. Which I don't." It's bad enough I dragged her into a case by asking her to look into him—through illegal means. I don't need her being any more involved in this. "So, please, don't ask again."

Anya sighs again, that same annoyed sound she's always used since childhood when she gets frustrated with me. "Vik, I'm worried about you. This isn't the kind of guy you want to tangle with."

"I can handle it. Handle *him*."

She snorts and chuckles. "I've heard that before."

I lean back in my chair and scan the squad room for anyone potentially eavesdropping. "I gotta go. But thanks for the info. This conversation never happened."

"Of course not. I'll keep digging, too, to see if I can find anything useful."

"Thanks."

I end the call and glance down the hallway toward the interrogation rooms. Still no sign of Hank, so he must be in there with Dixon. I flip on my computer screen to try to peek in on their conversation through the live feed, but the feed from the room I left our suspect in is black.

"What the hell?"

"Something wrong, Vik?" Pete peers over my shoulder at my screen.

I motion toward the blank screen. "I was trying to check on an interrogation, but the feed isn't showing anything."

Pete leans over and uses my mouse to click on another feed which instantly pops up, showing Detective Jacobson interrogating a suspect in a different room. "Looks like the other feeds are working. Maybe a malfunction on this one? Check the equipment."

Shit.

If Hank is having any success with Dixon, none of it will

be on video or audio, which makes it ten times harder if we bring a case to trial in the future.

I push away from my desk, head back toward the interrogation rooms, and almost run directly into Hank as he comes around the corner. "Did you get anywhere with Dixon?"

Hank stops and rubs the back of his neck, glancing behind me toward the squad room. "The guy stonewalled me just like he did to you."

"Well, I just got confirmation from a source that he *is* former Delta Force. It doesn't surprise me that he's being difficult. But maybe I can use that information to get under his skin."

"I let him go, Vik."

"What? Why the hell did you do that?"

I wasn't anywhere near done with that man, and we still don't have any of the answers we need. Given a bit more time, I might have gotten something useful out of that handsome hardass man.

Hank motions back toward the room where I sat across from Dixon not so long ago. "Because the littering charge was bullshit, and you know it. He would've gotten it dismissed if the DA even decided to charge it. And that's not the type of guy you want pissed off at you."

Anger tightens my hands into fists at my sides. "I could've broken him, Hank. I could've found out what he was doing at B66. What his interest is in all of this."

"I don't think that guy breaks for anything, Vik. Except maybe a deer in the road. Just let it go, and we'll continue our investigation."

What the hell? Let it go?

If I weren't standing right here and hadn't heard it with my own ears, I wouldn't believe those words just came out of

Hank's mouth. He's never been the type to let things go. Neither am I. It's why we've always worked so well as partners. We aren't willing to let things slip through the cracks.

But for some reason, he was willing to let Dixon go without getting any answers when we could have kept him at least a few hours longer and pushed him harder. The man never even asked for an attorney after we read him his rights and brought him in. We had free rein...at least for a little while longer. And Hank let him walk.

The blank footage flashes at the forefront of my mind. "I tried to watch the interrogation footage from when you were in with him, but it was blank. What happened?"

"Oh, yeah?" Hank glances behind him toward the room and rubs his neck again. "I couldn't get the equipment to work."

Bullshit.

In all the years we have worked together, I've never seen Hank so fidgety, averting his eyes, trying to brush off my concerns.

He's lying.

Whatever happened between Dixon and Hank in that room, he didn't want it recorded, and then he rushed our suspect out of here before I could question him again. That was intentional. There isn't any doubt in my mind.

The question is...why? Why would Hank help someone who is clearly involved in the shady shit happening at B66?

Hank's focus centers on something over my shoulder. "Shit. Sorry, Vik, Tiffany is here for some reason. I gotta go talk to her and make sure Brady is okay."

You have got to be fucking kidding me...

How convenient that his ex-wife appears right when I'm about to grill him for more answers about Dixon.

Hank is up to something, and whatever it is, it isn't good.

I never thought I'd say it, but I'm starting not to trust my own partner.

REAPER

I flick open my Zippo and light up a cigarette, but sucking in much-needed nicotine to my system doesn't help the growing frustration tensing my body. Detective Grayson let me go over twenty-four hours ago, and there still hasn't been any word from Kosofik. Plus, all I'm getting from my other sources in the city is dead end after dead end.

Whatever is happening with this auction, anyone who knows anything is staying tight-lipped. Which makes my mission nearly impossible. Typically, it's pretty easy to shake loose the information I need—sometimes with the use of force—but all I'm getting now is stonewalled no matter what I do.

It's possible my appearance at B66 sent out a warning signal to Yankovich's crew that made them lock down everything tightly and issue warnings against anyone who knew anything. But more likely, it was Detectives Grayson and Garin. They stood out like a damn lighthouse signaling "we don't belong here"—at least to me. And if any of Yankovich's men caught on, too, then they're sure to be in crisis mode.

I take a drag off the cigarette, close my eyes, and the image of the "menu" flashes against my lids, making me wince as if someone punched me straight in the gut.

The sounds of the city surround me out on the fire escape. Honking horns. Yelling. Laughter. With over twenty million people in the New York metropolitan area, finding those innocent women is going to be impossible without some help. Which means I need more boots on the ground, more people to help crack kneecaps and put the screws to anyone who might have any information about the auction or where I can find the girls.

And there are only two people I can trust to do that without a second thought. The men who have held my life in their hands while I have held theirs in mine. More like brothers than friends, they'll come without question and do whatever it takes. And when they learn about what's happening here and how my little favor for Cutter got me in this position, they'll show up armed and ready.

Yankovich and his crew are precisely the type of men we've spent years fighting against and taking out. The men who have caused us to lose other brothers and end up soaked in their blood. They're the people we've dedicated our lives to eliminating. So, they'll come. No question.

I drop my cigarette and grind it out with my boot on the metal stair below me as I dial Chaos. While it rings, I lean forward and rest my elbows on my knees, sucking in a breath of air filled with all the smells of those millions of people.

Chaos picks up on the second ring. "Yep."

"It's me. You busy?"

Something metal bangs in the background before the phone jostles and he returns. "I got a minute."

"I need you in New York. Going to text Mouth to see if he can come."

More jostling crackles through the line, then a heavy sigh I know better than to take personally. "I'm kind of in the middle of something. What's going on there?"

I run a hand through my hair and toss back my head to stare up at the night sky even though I can't see any stars here in the city. So different from so many places I've been, places with endless desert or jungle and no cities for hundreds of miles. "Cutter called and asked me to take care of an extermination in Manila."

Chaos chuckles low. "He told me about that last week when we talked. Sounds like it went well, though, so why do you sound so pissed?"

"That part of it did, but I learned we have a bigger vermin problem."

"Shit."

"Yeah." I fight back the memory of the girl I pulled from that trunk and what I did to Danilo to get the information that led me here. There isn't any need to get into specifics over the phone. Chaos and Mouth both know I wouldn't call if it wasn't important and necessary. "It's bad."

"What are we looking at?"

"A whole lot of vodka-drinking rats."

"Shit. I'm not sure how long this will take me to clean up."

"Just get here as quickly as you can. Things are complicated. There's...a woman cop who stuck her nose where it doesn't belong."

Chaos bites back a laugh. "A woman, huh? Never known you to get bent out of shape over a skirt."

"Yeah, well, you'll see why. Let me know when you're on your way."

"Stay out of trouble 'til I get there."

I bark a laugh and end the call, then immediately pull up my messages and fire one off to Mouth.

**Vermin problem in New York.
Need you here.**

Almost immediately, the three little dots that let me know he's replying pop up.

Give me a few days.

My chest tightens, and I rub at it with my free hand.
The girls might not have a few days.

Yankovich's auction could be happening right now, and I wouldn't have any fucking way of knowing. If Kosofik made me, he'll never send the message giving me the information, and the girls could be gone before I can even make a move.

All I can do is keep pounding the pavement and putting the screws to my sources, hoping something pans out while I wait for Chaos and Mouth to get here to help.

I'm just one man in a city of millions. But when they get here, the three of us together will be a force to be reckoned with. The Russians have no idea what's coming for them, and we will succeed. As long as Detective Grayson and his beautiful partner, Detective Garin, stay out of our way.

Grayson and I may share the same goal but teaming up with him will be the last resort. If I can't dig up anything useful in the next day or two, I'll see what he's willing to share with me.

Until then, I'm ready to do whatever it takes to find those girls and get them home safely—no matter how much blood I have to spill.

4

REAPER

"Fucking shit." I end the call, toss my phone into the center console, and slam my fist against the steering wheel before pulling out into traffic to make my way to the meeting I absolutely thought I would never fucking arrange. "Motherfucking hell!"

I can't believe I just called the damn cop.

Bringing Detective Grayson in on this goes against all my training. It could interfere with what I'm going to have to do. Having the fucking cops tagging along or inserting themselves will limit my actions in a way I can't afford. But after almost two days of digging until my fingers practically bleed, I still haven't been able to find out where Yankovich holds the girls, and Kosofik hasn't contacted me on the burner phone with a time and location. Yet, the rumor mill is still spouting off talk about an auction happening—and soon.

That means either Kosofik isn't ever going to give me the info—because he saw through my act or maybe saw the cops grab me outside—or that it will happen so last-minute that I won't be able to get in there and free the girls before the place is swarming with even more security *plus* scumbags there to buy them like cattle.

It means I'm getting desperate—something that never happens.

Time is ticking away for those girls. That's the only reason I called Detective Grayson and asked to meet him. Even with Mouth and Chaos agreeing to come to NYC to help me, it won't mean anything if we can't get a location on the girls. Mouth, Chaos, and I know how to follow through on a tough mission, so if Grayson doesn't have what I need, then I may have to resort to more bloody means of obtaining the information. But I worry that will only alert the men behind this that I'm coming for them. They'll move the girls and go into hiding before I can do anything. That would only make things worse for the victims.

Such a clusterfuck.

Even taking out Yankovich won't end this. As much as I'd love to believe that whole "take the head off the snake" bullshit, he has men like Kosofik who will step right up into his role and keep this sinister train moving. In order to *really* end this, we need to take them *all* out. And we can't do that if we can't fucking find them.

Something Detective Grayson can hopefully help with...

I pull up to the meet location at Roll N Roaster and park beside the building, scanning the streets on either side of the corner restaurant. The smell of frying oil smacks me in the face through my open window, turning my stomach, but not as much as the idea of what's happening to those girls does.

Detective Grayson climbs from a truck a few spots over and walks past my vehicle and toward the rear of the restaurant, apparently expecting me to follow him around the back. This late, it shouldn't be easy to spot us together, which is good for both of us given the circumstances.

Still surveying the area, I climb from the truck and make my way after the cop. The crisp fall air would be a lot nicer if I could smell anything other than the food from this place and the dirt of the fucking city.

I turn the corner to find him standing next to the dumpsters and grease traps, hands shoved into his pockets.

Fucking great. I guess I just won't breathe during this meeting.

He nods at me as I approach, then quickly scans the parking lot and street. "Glad you made the right choice, Dixon."

I snort and shake my head. "I haven't made *any* choice yet, Grayson. Don't take my request for this meeting as a statement that we're now buddies or that I plan on working with you on anything."

A scowl turns down his lips, and he takes a step toward me. "Then what the hell did you call me for?"

I shove a hand through my hair and check the small strip of street visible behind Grayson for anyone who might be close enough to hear anything we're discussing. This topic of conversation certainly isn't anything we want to share with members of the public. The area appears clear aside from a group of teenagers walking down the sidewalk away from the restaurant.

Still, I take a step closer to him, so I can keep my voice down. "If what you said at the precinct is true and we're looking for the same thing, then we have a real problem. My sources around town and here on the East Coast tell me an important auction is happening soon. Like *real* soon. And I have been striking out in terms of finding a location where I might be able to intercept the '*lots*' before they're sold to the highest bidder."

"Fuck. An auction?" He shifts and glances over his shoulder before returning his attention to me. "We knew they were trafficking, but an auction wasn't even on our radar."

"They're very well organized, which means we don't have a lot of time to fuck around."

"It also means Michail has flipped the fucking script."

I narrow my gaze on him. "If you know anything that could help me find them, I need you to tell me now. My hands aren't tied the way yours are. I can do whatever needs to be done. Nothing is off the table."

He considers me for a moment and opens his mouth like he's about to respond when the roar of motorcycle engines fills the night air around us, rumbling deep in my chest the closer they come.

What the hell?

Four bikes roll up on the street behind Grayson, and my hand automatically moves toward my weapon at my hip.

Grayson scopes out the new arrivals and holds up a hand while sliding his other into his pocket. "Hold it. They're with me."

I narrow my eyes at him and keep my hand exactly where it is. This doesn't feel right, and there's no way I'm letting down my guard when he's springing fucking surprises. For all I know, this fucker is setting me up to get taken out by these assholes so it won't tarnish his badge.

He wouldn't be the first dirty law enforcement officer I've come across, and he sure as shit won't be the last. Though, I don't believe for a second that Detective Garin knows what he's up to. She's too straight of a shooter. A rule follower. No way she knows he's meeting with me or is tied to a fucking motorcycle club.

Hand on my gun, I quickly check my back to ensure no one is coming around the other side. A brief flash of movement gives me pause, but the sound of advancing heavy boots makes me whirl back toward him. "Want to tell me what fuck is going on?"

"Hear me out." He turns to face me while the four guys climb off their bikes, the lights from the restaurant making their Satan's Knights patches visible on their cuts, and amble toward us. "They can help."

Even though every fiber of my being is telling me to hightail it back to my truck and out of here, the face of the girl I pulled from that trunk back in the Philippines flashes in my head. It's the only thing that keeps my feet cemented to the pavement.

Grayson motions toward the man at the front of the group of bikers. "This is Jack Parrish, the former president of the Satan's Knights."

Parrish gives me a dirty look and sneers. "Who the fuck are you?"

Like I'm going to tell this asshole anything.

I don't know what the fuck the cop is up to setting this meeting with these guys and not warning me, but I don't like it one fucking bit. These are the kind of situations that get you killed.

And these are the kind of men I don't offer anything to. "You can call me Reaper."

Grayson turns back to Parrish. "He's Delta Force. I brought you both here because I think the only way we're going to get this cunt is if we all work together."

Seems the detective knows more than I gave him credit

for about my history. Someone must have been doing some digging since I was released.

Grayson or his pretty partner?

Parrish fixes a glare at Grayson.

The cop seems undeterred by the threat in the look. "You got the past, but Dixon's got the present. Come on, Jack, do you really think I'd tell you to come here if I didn't think this guy was legit? He checks out."

Grayson may have checked me out, and I had Preacher run him before I ever made that call to set up this meeting, but I don't know anything about these guys except they're criminals—for all I know, he brought them here because they're involved in this whole fucking thing with the girls in the first place.

I keep my hand on my weapon. No matter how friendly or non-threatening they may appear to be at the moment— and really, they're both—these are the kind of men who can turn on you in an instant. It's easy to recognize someone so much like me, and I see it in every single one of these fuckers.

Parrish clucks his tongue against the roof of his mouth and steps to the side, allowing me to get a good look at the three men behind him. "This is Cobra—"

Pop! Pop! Pop!

Gunfire erupting from the street behind me interrupts the introductions, and I reach for my weapon and dive for cover.

VIKTORIA

Goddammit!

I wouldn't believe it if I weren't watching it unfold with my own eyes—Hank, Dixon, and the Satan's Knights... together. Conspiring. I didn't *want* to believe it. Yet, deep down, I *knew* Hank was up to something. This just confirms the uneasy feeling I've had for days since the minute he asked me to go to B66 and not start a formal investigation.

It was a red light flashing right in front of me, yet I ignored it because I *trusted* Hank. Because we were talking about the potential of there being innocent women out there who needed our help. Women we *couldn't* help without more information and actionable evidence. Then I allowed myself to brush off the unease because of the way Dixon got under my skin. I blamed it on the fact that he got me off my game. But I was right to suspect Hank was hiding something and lying to me.

Trusting my gut has never led me astray before, and I should have trusted it and confronted him right away—the moment he stepped out of the interrogation room and told me he let Dixon walk.

Going to B66 unofficially should have been enough to make me question it. His releasing Dixon should have been another nail in the coffin. And couple that with what I discovered after, what Hank had *done* to cover his own tracks, it was clear Hank has been keeping some serious secrets.

There's no way the video *and* audio feeds to the interrogation room just happened to malfunction while he was in there with our suspect. Not when they had been working perfectly fine when I was in there with Dixon only hours before...and continued to work fine when I tested them *after*.

The system was tampered with—intentionally—by the one person I'm supposed to be able to trust with my life on a daily basis. Whatever went down between the two of them in that room, Hank didn't want me to know about it.

And now, he's lied to me *again* and snuck out of the precinct—apparently to meet with a bunch of criminals.

What the hell is he doing with the Satan's Knights? And why the fuck *is Dixon here with all of them?*

The information Anya finally came through with this morning about Dixon let me know I was spot-on with my suspicions. He has seen some serious shit as a member of one of the world's most elite special forces groups.

You don't just walk on to Delta Force. They only recruit the best of the best, the cream of the crop, the most talented operators in the armed forces, which means that man is more dangerous than just about anyone on the planet. And not just because of his sexy smirk and striking blue eyes.

He's lethal and coupled with a dirty cop and a criminal MC, this is looking really fucking bad. The code he lived by in Delta must have stopped existing once he was discharged. It's not unheard of, I guess, going "bad" after serving time overseas and doing the kinds of things he likely had to. Men are changed when they live that way, do those things, and some of them come back lacking the basic ability to humanize. It can make them do things completely out of character.

But that idea just doesn't sit well in my stomach. Even with all the evidence otherwise, something tells me Dixon isn't the type of guy who would get involved in something shady. He has a *code*. Maybe not the same one they swear to when they're active duty. But he has one. One he *believes*.

One I can't see him breaking just to make some money off selling women.

A cop, a one-percenter motorcycle club, and a former Delta Force member walk into a bar...

It sounds like the start of a bad joke, and that's exactly what this is feeling like right now, watching it go down in front of me. If I could get closer, I might be able to overhear something that could shed some light on what's happening between these people who have no business being together. However, given where they're standing, I'm not sure I can without someone spotting me.

I need to try, though...

If I'm going to confront Hank about this, I need all the ammunition I can get. I need to know what they're up to, what they have planned. Because it may be worse than I even think. It isn't something I *want* to believe possible for a man I thought I knew almost as well as I know myself, but this could end our partnership. This may be something I need to go to IA about.

Shit. I hope not.

For better or for worse, Hank is my partner. He has my back, and I have his. That's why what he's been doing the last few days is so upsetting. Either it's so beyond what's right that he knows he could never tell me, or he doesn't trust me enough to fully fill me in. Both possibilities hurt more than I'd like to admit, twisting at my gut like I took a knife to it.

I need to know the truth. Here. Now.

Inching my way toward the group where they stand at the back of the restaurant, I stay low and against the building wall to try to maintain my cover. If they see me, I'll never get any answers. But I still can't hear what's being said and can only catch glimpses of them for a split second before I have to take cover again.

Desperate times call for desperate measures. I take a chance and dart from next to the wall to behind a large garbage can even closer to the group.

"You can call me Reaper." Dixon's deep voice reaches me, sending a shiver down my spine.

Reaper?

Hank's voice rises above the noise from the street. *"He's Delta Force. I brought you both here because I think the only way we're going to get this cunt is if we all work together. Come on, Jack, do you really think I'd tell you to come here if I didn't think this guy was legit? He checks out."*

All work together?

Hank wants to bring the Satan's Knights and Dixon in on taking down Yankovich. That explains the meeting, but it doesn't explain *why*. We could do this through proper channels, stake out the locations we *know* are connected to Yankovich until we see something we can use. We could pull in his guys until someone talks. We could do our *jobs* the way we're supposed to—legally and by the book. We could bring them down and ensure their faces are splashed across every paper in the country and they're exposed for what they're doing.

Before I can hear anything else that might answer my question, the sharp crack of gunfire shatters the night and a sharp slice of pain in my right side knocks me to the ground.

Agony blurs my vision as I try to search the street at the end of the alley for a shooter, and I struggle to reach for my gun at my side. My arm doesn't want to cooperate, but when I finally get it down there, my hand comes away covered in warm, sticky blood, and I collapse back against the concrete.

Shit.

The gunfire continues, seemingly coming from both the street and where everyone was meeting around the side of the building. The restaurant's position on the corner means they're exposed to attack on more than one side.

And I'm exposed here. The rounds ping off the concrete around me and the metal trash can behind me relentlessly while I lie on the damn ground, bleeding like a stuck pig. Which means no one is coming to help me. They can't. There isn't any way anyone could get here without getting hit, even if they wanted to and tried.

Given I wasn't invited to this little chat, my guess is no one will bother. If I'm going to get out of here alive, I need to do it myself.

Get the fuck up, Vik. Move!

I try to push myself up onto my elbow, but a searing burn sends me back down roughly, and I press my hand against the seeping wound at my side. Blood oozes out around my fingers, and darkness starts to encroach on the edges of my vision.

Stay awake. Don't close your eyes.

Gunfire grows closer.

Muffled yells.

A deep voice near my ear.

Someone over me.

"Fuck!"

Strong arms lifting me.

Squealing tires.

And then, nothing.

5

VIKTORIA

Strong arms close around me. The world spins. Something tightens around me. A warm palm presses hard against my side. Pain surges through my body, threatening to make me retch. The squeal of tires fills my ears. Voices bounce around my head. Honking horns. Broken conversations. Distorted words fade in and out with a darkness that threatens to completely drag me under.

A soft touch brushes the hair away from my face. All I want to do is lean into it...escape from the agony...

"She goes in and out of consciousness. The bleeding looks like it might be subsiding."

Dixon?

His words come from directly above me, his chest rumbling against me.

"And you?"

Hank?

"I'm fine." Annoyance and anger taint Dixon's clipped

response. "I'd be better if we got to wherever it is we're going, though."

Where are we going? Where are they taking me?

The movement stops, and I shift and groan at the pain that shoots through my side. But then I'm being lifted, jostled, though the arms I'm wrapped in try to cushion each movement.

Darkness reaches out to me again...

Angry voices...

Yelling...

"Can you people do this shit later?" Dixon issues a low growl of warning to someone. "She's starting to come to again."

My back hits something hard, and without the warm arms cradling me, the agony I was already in redoubles. I squeeze my eyes shut and cry out through clenched teeth, wrapping my arms around myself to try to hold my body together when it feels like it's shredding apart.

"Do you have anything to give her for the pain?" Hank snarls his question to whoever we're with.

"This ain't a fucking triage unit, man," someone hisses. "We don't got morphine; we got whiskey."

"Give it to her." Dixon's clipped order hits my ears.

"You heard the man." Hank's agreement has me turning toward his voice.

"Hank?" My voice comes out soft, full of all the agony I'm feeling.

"Right here, Vik." He pulls my hand into his and squeezes gently. The familiar touch and just knowing he's here relaxes me slightly...

Until someone unwraps something from around my waist and probes at the wound at my side.

Fuck!

I flinch and grit my teeth to keep from crying out or smacking away whoever it is, but I force open my eyes to meet Hank's. "I was shot."

"Yeah, you were, but you're going to be okay. Celeste is a nurse, and she's going to patch you right up."

"The good news is it looks like the bullet went straight through." The woman, who must be Celeste, lifts her focus from my side to meet my gaze and nods to a bottle in the hands of Jack Parrish, the notorious former president of the Satan's Knights. "Now might be a good time to give her some of that."

Shit. That doesn't bode well for me.

Hank slips his hand under my head and lifts it gently, bringing the bottle to my lips.

"What's this?" I probably shouldn't be blindly trusting what one of the Satan's Knights is giving me, especially someone with such a bad rep.

Hank smirks. "Whiskey. It'll help with the pain while she closes the wound."

I hesitate for a second, scanning the space around me through blurry vision. Lying shot and vulnerable in a room full of criminals isn't where I imagined I would find myself today. Every fiber of my being wants to run—to head to the precinct or the hospital to let the proper people know what's happened. But Celeste does something at my side that shatters any resistance I have, and I howl and wrap my hand around Hank's wrist to guzzle from the bottle.

"Whoa!" A redhead standing to the side of us raises her eyebrows. "I want to party with her one day."

After finally chugging what I hope is enough to slightly numb the pain, I push away Hank's hand and the bottle and settle my head back against the table. The movement coupled with the booze is enough to send my stomach rolling, and I wipe my mouth with my hand and take in all the people surrounding us while Celeste does something to the wound that sets my entire body on fire. The strange, mixed crowd brings back the memory of the conversation I overheard before the shooting started.

I glare at Hank while Celeste works on my side. "You want to tell me what the hell is going on? Why are you working with the Satan's Knights?" I glance over my shoulder to Jack Parrish. "No offense or anything. I appreciate the fake doctor performing surgery on me, and the whiskey is pretty potent, too."

"Only the best for our brothers and sisters in blue." Jack winks at me. "You should visit us when you're not shot and bleeding all over the place. We're a good time."

Un-fucking-likely.

I narrow my eyes on Dixon, who has remained suspiciously quiet, standing against the wall, taking in everything and everyone around him with a shrewd gaze, his bloody hand pressed against his upper arm. "And what's he doing here?"

"You're welcome." Dixon practically growls the words at me.

Scoffing, I raise an eyebrow at him. "Excuse me?"

What would I have to thank him for? Getting me shot?

"Maybe she should take another shot," the redhead suggests.

"Look, Vik…" Hank sets his hand on my arm. "I'll explain everything, but right now, you need to calm down. Here, take another swig."

Trying to get me drunk so I won't ask questions. No fucking way.

"Not until you start talking, Hank."

Something *major* is going on here. Major enough that

my own partner has blatantly lied to my face—repeatedly. Major enough that he's willing to risk his badge by meeting with the Satan's Knights and one of our suspects he released. Major enough that we got *shot at* and rather than report it and go to the hospital, he brought us wherever the fuck we are. He better have a damn fucking good explanation.

Hank sighs and runs a hand back through his hair. "Fine, Parrish is the one who gave me the intel on Yankovich. It wasn't an anonymous tip."

Before he can get another word out, the tray of supplies crashes to the floor, causing everyone to turn and stare at the redhead. She watches Hank with wide eyes. "I'm sorry, but did you say Yankovich?"

Two of the Satan's Knights guys rush to her side, and one pulls her into his arms and forces her to tear her shocked gaze away from Hank. Mumbled words reach me from across the room. He's telling her about Michail and the operation we suspect he's running.

"So Yankovich shot her?" the girl stammers, glancing back at me.

"We don't know who shot her, Ally," Parrish interjects. "But we're going to find out, and we're going to take down Michail just like we took out his brothers."

"Hold on." I try to push myself up but pain and Celeste's strong hand on my chest keep me down. "You're going to *take him out*?" I turn to Hank. "We're cops, Hank. We ride on the side of the law. What the hell are you doing?"

How can he think this is okay? That I can just let him help Parrish murder people?

Hank stares at me for a moment, the wheels churning in his head. "Vik, we took an oath to serve and protect the people in our community, but you know that sometimes even the good cops—hell, even the best—need help from the outside. We're not going to catch this guy on our own. We don't have the department backing us, and even if we did, it wouldn't change things." He pauses and turns to the blonde. "She's living proof the system is broken. If you don't believe me, ask her yourself."

"What the fuck are you doing?" Cobra—according to the name on his cut—snaps. "Ally's been through enough shit. She ain't reliving it to ease your conscience or your partner's."

"Jagger," Ally calls, placing a hand on his arm. It must be his real name—confusing as fuck when you're in massive amounts of pain. "It's okay."

"No, it's not." The other member who comforted her earlier, Deuce, shakes his head. "Cobra is right. This ends here, or you can patch your girl up yourself."

"Both of you need to quit it," Ally shouts. "I can decide what I want to share and what I don't. That's the beauty of being rescued. I get to be my own person again, and you two need to stop hovering." She turns and looks at Hank for a moment, then focuses on me. "Your partner is right; the system failed me. I was fourteen years old walking from the neighborhood pizzeria when a white van pulled up to the curb. A man rolled down his window, and he appeared distraught. He said he had a daughter my age and that she was missing. At the time, all I could think of was my dad. If something had happened to me, I wouldn't want him roaming the streets, begging people to help him find me, so I got inside his car. The man was Vladimir Yankovich. It didn't take long for me to realize my mistake. As soon as he put the full-face helmet over my head, blocking out my cries for help, I knew I was done. I stopped praying for someone to rescue me and started wishing my death would be quick and painless."

"Fucking hell," Cobra hisses.

"I was forced to give a blow job before I ever even had my first kiss. I was used and abused, and then I was sold to a man just as vile as Yankovich, and that guy turned me into a junkie. He kept me a prisoner for years. My parents..."

"Ally, baby, come on." Cobra reaches out to her, but she brushes off his touch. "You don't have to do this."

She shakes her head and keeps her focus on me. "My parents never gave up on me. They gave all their trust and all their faith to the detectives in charge of my case, but they never found me. They never even named Yankovich as my captor. When my case went cold, my dad hired a bounty hunter." Her gaze cuts to Hank. "Your dad."

Hank shoves his hands into his pockets and nods.

Keeping her eyes locked with mine, she sighs and continues. "He is the one who put two and two together and realized Yankovich had taken me, but by then, it was too late. I was already in Rush's possession, and Yankovich had killed my parents." She pauses and lifts her gaze to Jack, the corners of her mouth curling as she gives him a sad smile. "If it weren't for Rick Grayson and the Satan's Knights, I'd be dead." She turns back to me. "I don't know what the hell is going on, but if this Michail guy is anything like his brothers, you need all the help you can get because if even one innocent girl slips through the cracks, that's on you. Will you be able to live with that weighing on your conscience for the rest of your life?"

Well, shit.

As if the physical pain of being shot and then poked and prodded by Celeste isn't bad enough, Ally's story certainly makes this a lot more complicated and painful.

In this job, there's a line I don't want to cross, one that would bring me into that gray area that leads even further into the blackness that turns so many good cops bad. I've always prided myself on staying on the right side.

But here, there isn't one. Not when innocent women are being sold like cattle and abused in ways I can't fathom. Hank is right that we'll be restricted by the badges we wear, by the very law we fight so hard to uphold and enforce.

That truth weighs heavily on my chest as I let Celeste finish patching me up, alternating between clenching my eyes shut to keep from throwing up and locking gazes with Ally, Hank, and Dixon.

When my "doctor" finishes and finally steps back, I inhale a long, deep breath and blow it out before looking at my partner again. "I'll keep this quiet from the department. For *now*. But only because I know they'd pull us both off duty and probably fire you for working with the MC."

Hank nods his agreement. "Probably." He glances around the room at the members of the Satan's Knights and still-quiet Dixon. "But working together, I think we can all get this fucker and ensure no more innocent women suffer like Ally did."

I sure as hell hope so because if we fail, we won't be able to explain away what's already happened. We'll lose our badges, our jobs, and we could end up in prison ourselves if we have to do what I think we will. Squeezing my eyes closed, I try to force all the worst-case scenario possibilities to the back of my head. If I dwell on them too much, I might do something I will regret, something that could get those girls killed or worse.

Releasing a deep breath, I open my eyes and meet Hank's concerned gaze. "I'm in. I'll call in sick for a few days at work so no one suspects anything, but for now, I just want to go home, Hank. Drive me?"

Hank raises an eyebrow. "Home? No, you should stay here a while. Let Celeste watch you and make sure you're okay."

I shake my head and grit my teeth as I try to sit up and fail miserably. "I'll be fine. Just get me to my apartment. Give me a few days to recover while you all figure out the specifics of our plan."

He looks ready to argue with me, and when I look to where Dixon has been leaning against the wall, the spot is empty. I scan the rest of the room, but he isn't anywhere in sight.

Where the hell did he go?

It doesn't matter. I'm too exhausted to worry about where that brooding man ran off to at this moment. Even if the memory of his touch, the way he held me in the car on the way here, the soft brush of his fingers across my skin still warm me more than the whiskey ever could.

REAPER

The total darkness surrounding me might make some people uncomfortable, but I've embraced the dark for so long, it's more of a home than anywhere else in this world. I've never stayed anywhere long enough to make it feel like one, and darkness can be found anywhere, everywhere, really. It makes it easy to come back to it whenever I want.

But this is different. Because of *her*. Even in the pitch black, her light flowery scent permeates the air, invading my lungs with every breath. The feel of her limp in my arms weighs heavily on my chest. Her whimpers of pain ring in my ears.

I absently flip the top of my lighter, the rhythmic motion so familiar, it takes me back to another place. Another time. When I was doing the same thing in a dark room, surrounded by my brothers in arms. Before the whole thing went to shit.

Flashes of light and booms that shook the entire building still rattle through my body even now, and I clamp my hand around the lighter so hard that it hurts. But I barely realize I'm doing it until a key slides into the lock, breaking through the memory and the absolute silence of the room I had been enjoying prior to the past rearing its ugly head.

The deadbolt clicks, the sound echoing through the room seemingly as loud as the explosion that shook that night, and the door pushes in slowly, allowing in a sliver of bright fluorescent light from the hallway. It cuts across the hardwood floor, but before it can reach me and reveal my presence, Viktoria closes the door behind her and sags back against it with a grimace I can see even in the dark.

She sucks in several deep, painful-sounding breaths mixed with groans before pushing off the door and staggering forward. Her legs wobble, and she reaches out for a side table but misses, her hand finding nothing but air. She starts to fall forward, but I rise from the chair I've been sitting in for the last half an hour and grab her before she can hit the hard floor and injure herself further.

"What the fuck?" Viktoria jerks her head back to see who caught her and tries to yank herself from my grasp, but I tighten my hold on her upper arms.

Gritting my teeth, I bite back the torrent of curses that want to flow out at her jerking movements that are the last thing she should be doing after being shot and patched up haphazardly at an apartment above a fucking bar. "Stop fighting me, Viktoria, or you're going to end up face-first on the damn floor."

The blood loss she suffered tonight will be affecting her for a while, making her weak and unstable on her feet. She should have stayed at the clubhouse so Celeste could watch her for at least another day or two and ensure she rebuilt her strength before coming home alone. But Viktoria is far too stubborn to admit when she's weak and needs help. This woman would rather go down in flames than acknowledge a little smoke.

She freezes, her eyes finally adjusting to the darkness enough for them to focus up on me. Her bow lips twist into a scowl, and she tries to pull free from my hold again, though with far less fight in her—either because she doesn't have the energy anymore or because she knows I'm not a real threat. "Reaper? What the hell are you doing in my apartment?"

"Apparently, keeping you from face-planting."

Her lips press together in a hard line, her body tensing. "I could have *killed* you!"

I snort and shake my head, which only adds fuel to the fire dancing in her gaze. "Unfuckinglikely since you can barely stand up."

As if to prove me wrong, she tries to yank her arms from my hands, but she only manages to hurt herself—the exertion and twisting movement likely pulling at her stitches. She grits her teeth and winces, then takes a long, slow deep breath, trying to regain her composure.

"Get out." She lifts her head and scans the apartment behind me. "How the hell did you get in here, anyway? Or know where I live, for that matter?"

Too fucking easily.

After I slipped away from everyone at the club, I called Preacher to find Viktoria's address. In less than two minutes, I had what I needed and was in a cab on the way here to ensure I cleared the place before she came home.

And getting in was a piece of fucking cake.

The fire escape leading right up to the window of her bedroom couldn't be a greater invitation to someone with ill intent, and the ancient lock on the old wooden frame didn't last twenty seconds, allowing me to easily climb right into her most intimate space.

If I had been here for any other reason, she'd be dead or worse by now.

"You need better security."

"*You* need to leave." Her voice holds firm conviction but underlying it, a tiny waver brought on by her weak physical state, belies her deep fears, the ones she doesn't want to acknowledge. The fact that if someone did break in right now, she wouldn't be in *any* shape to defend herself against an attack.

I drop my head until my eyes align with her unfocused green ones, ensuring she sees the conviction there. "Not a chance in fucking hell, sweetheart."

She glares at me, her lips twisting again. "Do I need to call Hank to have him physically remove you?"

Like he could.

"Hank would agree with my being here to watch over you—I'm fucking confident of that. And I'm not leaving anytime soon because I'm worried about you, and not just because this place is a shithole with zero security that anyone could basically just walk right into if they wanted to hurt you."

"Why would anyone want to hurt me?" Her gaze darts

down to where my hands grip her upper arms, probably a little too hard.

Point taken.

I relax my hold on her slightly, waiting to release her until I'm confident her legs aren't going to give out from under her. She wobbles slightly, squeezing her eyes together, and reaches out for me to stabilize herself. Her hands press against my chest, and a rush of heat spreads out through my body from the point of contact like a fire has been lit over my heart.

Shit.

"I'm-I'm fine, Reaper." She drops her head and sucks in a painful breath. "Go."

Damn stubborn woman.

"You're not fine, Viktoria. Not by a longshot."

This woman clearly has no clue what's going on. She's a good, observant cop, who saw through me at B66 in an instant, yet she somehow managed to miss what was completely obvious to me.

"Do you really not know you were the target in that shooting tonight?"

Her head snaps up, her green eyes wide. "What? No. That doesn't make any sense. Why would anyone shoot at me?"

"That's a good fucking question we need to answer. It could just be someone you arrested who got out trying to get a little payback, or it could be something more." Like maybe the Russians made her at the club the other night and want her gone before she can interfere with what they're planning. "Until we figure it out, I'm not leaving you alone."

A low, tiny growl rumbles in her chest, anger flashing in her gaze despite the fact that she's about ready to pass out. "I don't need you protecting me, *Reaper*." She tosses my nickname at me like she's firing a bullet. "I can take care of myself."

The words barely leave her lips before she winces and reaches down to press her right hand against her side. When she pulls it away, blood covers her palm, and a dark-red stain spreads across the fabric of her shirt.

Shit. Now she's really done it.

No doubt Viktoria is a strong woman who is good at her job, but if I hadn't jumped in to shield her during the shooting and then drag her out of there, she'd be dead. And if I weren't holding her up right now, she'd likely be spending the night on the floor, bleeding out.

"Like hell, you can." I scoop her up before she can object, ignoring the twinge of pain in my arm where I was hit and the little gasp of surprise slipping from her lips. "You're dead on your feet, and you're bleeding again."

She opens her mouth to object but then winces and wraps her arms around my neck. Either she's given up on arguing with me, or her body is doing it for her. It doesn't matter to me, as long as she stops fighting. The more she does, the worse it will be for her.

I easily carry her to the bedroom, the dead weight of her body in my arms enough to drag up memories I'd rather keep buried. Ones I managed to push away when she returned home.

This isn't that.

No matter how many times I try to remind myself that that's true, it doesn't stop the anxiety that tightens my chest. I'm no longer in a war zone, but the truth is, I just traded one type of war for another. All I've ever been is a soldier. The only skills I possess gave me the name Reaper, and now, I have no choice but to use them to do what's right—no matter how difficult. I just never expected a complication like this beautiful, feisty woman getting in my way.

I lower her to the bed and pull away the blood-stained shirt from her side, pushing it up around her breasts. Several of the stitches Celeste put in have come out. Not because Celeste did a bad job but because Viktoria is too damn stubborn. She should've stayed. They could have protected her and watched over her while she healed and was well enough to actually come back here.

But it seems she has to fight everyone on everything. And something tells me she's going to fight me the whole way, too.

It's a good thing I thrive in war.

6

REAPER

"Take off your shirt." My words come out gruffer than I had intended, but the frustration building with every argument that comes from her mouth is starting to bubble to the surface of my usually cool demeanor.

I've always prided myself on my ability to remain unaffected in *any* situation—it's one of the things that made me so good at my job. But this woman...

Christ, this woman...

She brings out something I didn't even know existed. I've always protected my brothers in combat, and doing Cutter this favor means putting myself in the line of fire for the innocent women being trafficked. But Viktoria is something else.

This *need* to decimate anyone who would even *think* of laying a hand on her seems to want to overpower my reason in this situation, and I'm fighting a losing battle against giving in to my base needs right now.

Her eyes widen at my command, and her mouth drops open with a surprised gasp. "What?"

Ignoring her indignation, I push off the bed and duck into the small bathroom to gather what I need to clean her up. I'd rather not have to drag her back to Celeste, and I managed to patch up my own arm when I got here with what little Vik had in her cabinets. God knows I've handled a lot worse injuries than ours—more times than I care to count.

"I *said* take off your shirt."

"Uh, no. I'm fine—"

I duck my head back into the bedroom and point at her. "No, you're not *fine*. Take off that *bloody* shirt so I can get you cleaned up, or I'll come take it off for you."

She scowls at me from where she sits propped up against the headboard. "You wouldn't!"

A low growl slips between my clenched teeth before I can bite it back. "Fucking try me, Vik."

Her hands fisted at her sides, she looks ready to argue again, but I narrow my eyes at her, giving her my best "you better not even think about it" look, silencing her immediately. Maybe she'll stop fighting me for five fucking seconds.

Or maybe Hell will freeze over.

Something tells me that would be more likely than Detective Garin just relaxing and letting me take care of her without opening that pretty mouth of hers with backtalk.

Returning from the bathroom, I almost step on the bloody shirt in a pile on the floor—probably tossed there with spite—and let my gaze travel up to her exposed skin and a lacy black bra that barely contains her breasts.

Fuck.

My cock twitches against my jeans even though this is clearly not the time nor the place for it to be making an appearance. But it's been a long fucking time since he came out to play, and Viktoria is a strikingly beautiful woman, even in her current state.

I'd have to be blind not to notice the way the light from the bedside lamp shimmers on her almost flawless pale skin —marred only by the nasty bleeding wound at her side— and the way her breasts swell and rise over the cups of that delicate bra with each huffy breath she takes.

Too bad she's pissed and injured because I can think of a few ways to help relieve some of the pain and stress from this day—for both of us.

She doesn't make eye contact with me, just stares out the window into the night with anger turning down her lips as I sit on the edge of the bed next to her and set down the supplies I found. It isn't ideal, but I'm used to making do with what's on hand in shittier places than this.

I tuck a towel under her side, grab the hydrogen peroxide, and pour it over the reopened wound.

She jerks her head toward me, gritting her teeth. "What the hell?"

Her natural response is to try to pull away from me, but I press a firm hand against her hip, holding her in place. "We need to make sure it stays clean before I close you back up."

Those green orbs dip down to the gauze I have pressed against her side, blood already seeping through it. "Shit." She shoves at my shoulder and tries to push my hand out of the way to take the gauze. "I can take care of this. Go."

"Like hell, you can. If I hadn't been here, you'd be out there napping in blood on the fucking floor. If not worse."

She tries to shift to sit up more, but I press my hand against her exposed chest, forcing her back. My fingers linger against the warm, soft skin there a little too long, but for some reason, I can't drag them away, and she doesn't make me.

Our eyes lock. Something sizzles between us. Something *other* than the anger and annoyance that has seemed to be constant since we first met outside B66. Something far more dangerous than either of those things.

I swallow thickly. "Let's get one thing straight, Vik. I'm not going anywhere until I'm sure you're safe."

"Safe?" She searches my face for something, but she isn't going to find it. It died a long time ago.

I pull my hand away from her chest and the other from her wound and examine the damage. "I'm going to have to re-close this."

She glances down. "With what?"

I hold up a needle and thread I found in her linen closet next to the bathroom.

Her eyes widen. "You can't use that."

"Watch me. I've used worse to close wounds a hell of a lot nastier than this." And the same setup worked just fine on my arm an hour ago when I arrived. Luckily, she seems to have a lot of sewing supplies.

She huffs and narrows her eyes on where I work to tie off the thread. "And they probably died from infection."

I grit my teeth and finalize the knots. "It wasn't from infection. And they didn't all die."

Just most of them.

Thinking about the number of friends I've lost over my last fifteen years in the service would only further heat my blood and drag me to that painful abyss at the bottom of a bottle I refuse to go back to.

She rests her hand over mine, and I glance up to find her soft gaze filled with compassion. "I'm sorry. I didn't mean—"

"It's fine." I cut her off before she can try to do any more digging into my psyche. Nothing good ever comes from that. I grab the prescription bottle I brought from the bathroom. "Found this in the medicine cabinet. You should take one."

It looks like she wants to say something else. Her lips open and close again before she accepts the bottle from me. "Vicodin. Left over from when I had my wisdom teeth pulled last year."

"This isn't going to feel very good, and you're going to be in a lot of pain the next couple of days. You'll want some of those. Though, be careful."

"You sound like you're talking from experience."

I freeze and glance up at her, trying my best not to give anything away. This woman has already gotten under my skin; the last thing I need is her delving any deeper into my soul or my weaknesses. "You could say that."

Her gaze drops to the bottle in her hand, and she removes the lid and pops one into her mouth, swallowing it with no problem, even without water. An uncomfortable silence stretches between us as she rolls the bottle in her palm. "I-I know you were Delta Force. I can only imagine what you must have seen and—"

"And that's exactly why you should listen to me when I tell you you're in danger."

She shakes her head. "I don't understand why you think that."

I nudge her to get her to lie back, then position the needle to make the first stitch. She nods that she's ready. Maybe if I keep her talking, the pain won't be so bad for her.

"Vik, those guys didn't start shooting until you showed up. You and I were the only two hit for a reason—because *you* were what they were aiming at and I covered you and got in the damn way."

I shove the needle into her skin and through to the other side of the wound.

She grinds her teeth together and sucks in a breath. "I suppose you want me to thank you for that."

Fucking smartass.

I make another stitch in silence, letting her comment hang in the air between us. Another one should close her back up and prevent any more bleeding. And I'd be lying if I said I wasn't enjoying the little jab of pain she's feeling with each stitch more than I probably should.

Some might call me a sadist, but it's not that I get off on causing her pain. I just know that it often helps me focus and see things I might not when my mind is clouded with other thoughts. Focusing on the pain means ignoring the other shit in my head. If that's true for Vik, too, she might be able to see what I'm trying to protect her from.

Finally done, I lean back and set everything on the nightstand before I examine my work. Not half-bad considering the circumstances and the less-than-cooperative patient.

Viktoria finally relaxes slightly and releases a long, slow breath. She keeps her eyes closed and her head dropped back against the headboard. It gives me an opportunity I don't need to stare at her perfect breasts in that damn tiny piece of lace that barely covers her nipples. As it is, the almost sheer fabric shows them reacting to the slight chill in the fall air, letting them poke out toward me.

My fingers itch to reach out and twist them as much as my mouth waters, thinking about sucking on them and lapping at them with my tongue.

Fucking hell...Not again.

To keep myself from touching her, I adjust my swelling

cock and rest my hand on the mattress near her leg to nudge her. "So, about that thank you."

VIKTORIA

Is he for real?

I open my eyes and watch him where he sits just to my right on the edge of my mattress. One of his dark eyebrows rises, waiting for some sort of response from me while amusement dances in eyes that seem to see all the way into my soul, to that part of me that wants to throw caution to the wind and do something that feels good even though it's so, so bad, for once.

Heat creeps up my leg where it touches his wrist and makes its way straight to my core. Like fire licking across my skin, it creeps over my exposed breasts, up my neck, and to my cheeks the longer he looks at me with that damn smirk.

No. No. No. No! This is not happening, Vik.

It doesn't matter how handsome he is or how strong the desire to climb him like a fucking tree might be. I can*not* be attracted to this man. He's a killer. An assassin trained by the damn government. He literally came to town to *murder* people. Bad people—but still...*murder!*

He's the kind of person I've fought hard to get away from, leads the kind of life I never wanted. I can't trust him to do what's right. He's always going to do whatever he wants, whatever he can justify in his own head, even if it's wrong and may hurt someone else.

Mainly me.

As soon as we take down this trafficking ring, he'll be gone again, off gallivanting around the world, doing whatever the hell it is he's doing now that he's retired. I don't even want to think about it—about what a man with his skillset does with them once his actions are no longer sanctioned by Uncle Sam.

The word *mercenary* keeps coming to mind, but even that feels wrong. With a name like Reaper, my guess is he's too good for a word like that.

"I'm not going to thank you, *Reaper*."

His other eyebrow wings up to join its counterpart. "Oh, yeah? Why not? That's kinda rude."

I scowl at him and cross my arms over my exposed chest, suddenly *very* aware of how nearly naked I am on top. "Because I wouldn't have gotten shot at in the first place if it weren't for you showing up in town and stirring shit up."

He barks out a laugh and shifts closer to me until his side presses against my thigh. "How do you figure that?"

"Hank and I had things under control at B66. We would have found out what we needed to through *legal* means and had everyone involved locked up within a few weeks."

"A few weeks?" He snorts and shakes his head. "Sorry, sweetheart, but that wasn't going to happen. If I could make you two as cops that easily, so could any one of Yankovich's guys. You two were never going to get anything or get anywhere close to wherever they're holding those girls. I'm the only chance they have."

I shake my head and try to ignore the desire to lean closer to him and the warmth he radiates. "I don't believe that. Even if they did make us, we would have used our sources and resources to find the girls. We don't have to resort to killing people."

"Sometimes that's what it takes to get the job done, Vik. I only do what I do because the authorities are either useless or have their hands tied."

Anger flares through my blood, and I lean forward with a slight wince. Despite the drugs taking the edge off the pain and making the world a little foggy around me, I'm still feeling what happened today. "So, I'm useless? We should just let vigilantes run around killing whoever they deem to be worthy of a death sentence?"

Reaper moves even closer, his shoulder almost touching my breast, and he reaches up to brush a strand of my hair away from my face.

The memory of the same soft touch after I was shot and was bouncing in and out of consciousness sends a shudder of anticipation through my body.

"You're far from useless, Vik. But your hands are tied by the badge you wear, and some people deserve death for what they do. It's as simple as that."

Is it really?

It's not something I ever considered at length before. Growing up, all I knew was I wanted a different life and was determined to make it for myself, one free of the crime and drugs and sketchy behavior that ran so rampant in my neighborhood. I was able to break away from it, but Anya wasn't so lucky, or more accurately, she just didn't care enough to do it. She was content to do dirty work—at least digitally—for anyone willing to pay her. And while I appreciate her entrepreneurial spirit and ability to use her skills to make a living, it's certainly not what I would have chosen for her.

But at least she isn't doing what *he* does. She isn't out there pulling the trigger and being the judge, jury, and executioner.

"I can't let you just go around killing people, Reaper. I took an oath. It's my job to uphold the law."

He raises a dark eyebrow at me. "Yet, you had no

problem breaking it by lying about the shooting and hiding your injury from the department?"

Guilt climbs like acid up my throat, and I have to swallow past it to respond. He called me out, brought to the surface the things I've been trying to justify in my own head. "That's different."

Reaper snorts and crosses his arms over his chest. "So, you pick and choose when you get high and mighty?"

"We're talking about *murder*, Reaper. You want to go in there, guns blazing, and kill anyone who gets in your way. We should be letting the police know where the girls are and where the auction is happening if we find out so they can come in and make arrests. Those men should have their day in court. They should go to prison and face justice."

His jaw clenches, anger blazing in his blue eyes, darkening them in a way that sends another shiver through me, though this one is different than before because I see the *real* danger staring right back at me. "I *am* justice. They're getting exactly what they deserve, and I'll do whatever it takes to make sure those innocent women are free and can't ever get hurt by bastards like Yankovich and his men again."

Before I can open my mouth to argue with him, he leans in, pressing his hands onto the bed on either side of my hips, making me sink back even farther into the mattress.

His warm breath flutters over my face, the heat of his body radiating into mine while anger rolls off him in waves. "I can't stop, Vik, and I won't let anything or *anyone* get in my way."

If Reaper thinks I'm going to back down on this, he couldn't be more wrong. But with him this close, it's hard to think of anything but grabbing him and pulling him even tighter against me, despite my injury. My body doesn't seem to care how weak I might be or that my inhibitions might be suppressed slightly by the damn Vicodin. Every part of me still yearns for his touch, his mouth, his hands...

Something about this man drives me wild—in the best and the worst ways. But the truth of who and what he is prevents me from acting on what I may want. While we share the goal of having these trafficking scumbags pay, we're on opposite sides when it comes to how to handle this fight.

I swallow thickly and try to stop myself from shaking before I respond to him. "Is that a threat?"

Reaper shifts even closer, his lips a mere hairsbreadth from mine. "No, sweetheart, that's a promise. One I intend to keep."

He brushes his mouth against mine, slow and soft at first, but when I release a tiny gasp and open my lips for him, he growls low and captures my face in his palms, angling my head up and allowing him to sweep his tongue inside and against mine.

I should push him away. I should say *no* and remind him I'm hurt and we're arguing and on opposite sides of the law, but I don't want to. Because Reaper has come unleashed. That control he exhibited in the interrogation room is gone, and all that passion we've been arguing with seems to now be focused on this kiss. The one that's stolen my breath completely.

When he finally pulls away, he shifts back and off the bed. "But I'm also going to keep you safe. Whatever it takes."

Whatever it takes to keep me safe.

The words should be comforting, knowing someone has my back and is protecting me. But somehow, it feels like even more of a threat.

7

VIKTORIA

Somehow, I managed to fall asleep after what went down with Reaper the other night. It was likely the mix of physical exhaustion, adrenaline dump, and the narcotics he made me take that finally did me in.

The last thing I remember is Reaper's hard eyes watching me like a hawk from where he sat in the little chair in my bedroom while I fought against heavy eyelids.

And when I woke yesterday morning...he was gone.

No sign of him. Not a single drop of blood. All the supplies and evidence of his patch-up job on himself and me vanished as if he were never even here in the first place.

It shouldn't surprise me. Not given his background. He's trained to disappear into the shadows without leaving a trace of his presence. But there was one thing he couldn't erase...the feel of his lips pressed against mine.

I reach up and brush my fingers over the exact place he kissed me. Even in pain and with the meds starting to take effect, that moment lives in vivid memory, almost like I can still taste him. Even after more than a day and half since he was here, his scent still invades my every breath.

Shit.

This man is turning into a major complication—personally and professionally. What I told him before he disappeared was true. I won't let him run off to slaughter Yankovich and his men without definitive proof they're doing what we think they are, and if it is at all possible to save the women caught up in the trafficking ring while still sending the men through the proper court process, I'll leap on that before I accept vigilante justice at the hands of Reaper, the MC, or anyone else.

And if I'm going to get in any deeper with this plan, I need to know exactly what and who I'm working with. Hopefully, Anya can provide me with some of that when we meet for lunch today, more than the very basics she was able to uncover initially.

I'll just need to be careful meeting her to ensure no one else sees me out and about, not after calling in and taking a few days off. It definitely raised some eyebrows with the boss, but better he not expect me for a couple days and be annoyed at my absence than be searching for me.

The way I'm still feeling today, even after resting and staying in bed all day yesterday, it would be difficult to hide that something is very wrong. Pain still slices at my side every time I move, and while Celeste and Reaper did an excellent job patching me up, the packing around the wound still bears the evidence of my injury—pale red seeping through in spots.

Shit.

I do my best to clean it up again, wincing and gritting my teeth when I lift my arm. My phone buzzes on the counter, and I glance down at the screen and the text from Hank I've been expecting after he checked in with me around the same time yesterday.

You doing okay today?

I'm good. See you in a few days. Keep me updated on anything urgent.

Will do. Call me if you need me.

I won't. At least, I wouldn't admit it to Hank—or anyone else, for that matter—if I did need help.

It was bad enough I had to rely on the MC to patch me up when I was shot and then Dixon to save me from ending up on my ass when I came home that night, so I don't have any plans to end up in that vulnerable position again.

Reaper seems to think I was the target of the shooting, but I'm far from convinced. It's more likely I was just in the wrong place at the right time and Dixon or someone from the MC was the real target. Getting caught in the crossfire makes more sense than someone targeting me out of the blue.

But still, I'll watch my back as best I can before I rely on someone else to do it again. While I can understand why Hank did what he did, he's broken a trust I'm not sure can ever be repaired.

I'll see this case through to ensure those girls don't suffer. But when the smoke clears, I may have to reevaluate where I stand with my partner.

There isn't any time to dwell on it now, though. I only have half an hour until I have to meet Anya. Which means I need to get moving even though I want to crawl back into bed and binge watch something sappy on Webflix.

I don't have that luxury today. Not if I want answers about the man who let himself into my apartment the other night and who left an indelible mark on my memory with that damn kiss.

My body heats just thinking about how close he was. How his large, calloused hands felt against my soft skin. The way his lips pressed into mine with a force that left the message undeniable—he doesn't intend to go down without a fight, and he won't disappear just because I don't want or need his protection.

That means even though he was gone when I woke this morning, he won't be for long. I need to get to my meeting with Anya before Reaper does something to interfere.

I slide on my jacket, wincing at the pull on my side, slip out the door, and lock it behind me. The hallway is silent this time of day—everyone is either gone at work or engrossed in their soap operas.

The elevator ride down seems to take forever, the ancient, creaky car shifting in a way that always makes my stomach lurch into my throat even after five years of living in this damn building. They'll never fix it, no matter how many times I complain, so it's just one of those little quirks of living in an old building in New York I have to live with.

So is the polluted air that hits me the moment I step out onto the busy sidewalk. Exhaust from traffic. Smoke from pedestrians' cigarettes and vapes. It makes me pause and cough, and I have to grab my side and clench my jaw to keep from crying out at the pain and drawing unnecessary attention to myself.

After a few deep breaths, I'm finally able to right myself and step out into the flow of people walking back and forth, always in a hurry.

The restaurant is only a few blocks down. Close enough

that I was sure I could make it no matter how shitty I might feel. Each step seems like more and more work, though. As if my shoes are weighted and my body is failing.

Dammit.

Being weak like this pisses me the fuck off. I became a cop so I could be in control and always be able to protect myself. But now, it feels like every set of eyes is on me, every car is slowing to stare, every person on the street might be a source of danger.

I'm letting Reaper get into my head now. That can't happen.

I shake off the paranoia creeping into the edges of my mind. I'm almost there. The restaurant is only half a block up on the opposite side of the street. Even from here, Anya's crimson bob is visible at one of the tables on the front patio.

The stoplight changes to red, and I pause, waiting for the sign to change. A tall man in a black peacoat steps up next to me. His dark gaze darts over to me briefly, and a shiver rolls through my spine.

The light changes, and I let him cross the street in front of me to the opposite corner where he turns right when I need to cross another street to the left to finally reach the restaurant. With her back to me, Anya hasn't seen me coming yet, but I spot the waitress chatting with her as I wait for yet another light change.

Almost there.

It will feel so good to sit down for a bit. I never could have anticipated how wiped out I'd be after such a short walk.

The light changes to green, and I step off the curb. A hand closes over my mouth and a strong arm wraps around my shoulders, dragging me back and toward a white van to the right before I can even react.

My instincts kick in immediately, and I reach back to try to eye-gouge my attacker, but somehow, he manages to shift his head away and wrangle me toward the open rear sliding door.

Don't let him get you into the van. Don't let him get you into the van.

But it's too late.

Strong arms maneuver me into the vehicle, and a black hood is shoved over my head as I kick out and swing wildly with my fists. My foot connects with something—someone —and a muttered curse fills the space, but before I can act again, my ankles and wrists are bound by skilled hands.

The van shakes with my captor's movements, and tires squeal as we move away from the curb at a breakneck pace.

Shit. So much for watching my back.

REAPER

Watching Viktoria make her way down the sidewalk, caught up in the throngs of people on their way to and from lunches and appointments, makes my stomach turn. Combined with my knee that won't stop bouncing wildly under the steering wheel, I am feeling decidedly unsteady compared to the other hundreds of times I've surveilled someone.

She couldn't have just stayed in bed another few days?

At least in her apartment, I know she's safe—relatively speaking. Nailing her bedroom window shut might have been overkill, but it was the only way to know for sure she wouldn't become the victim of someone who figured out how easy it was to get in, just as I had. She was so messed up when she got home that night, she hadn't even noticed I had done it, though I imagine the first time she goes to open it, there will be a few curses thrown my way.

But it's only a temporary fix for the greater problem—which is figuring out who wants her dead.

I need more time. Time to get fucking help here, time to look into why she would be the target for someone, time to locate the girls before this damn auction happens. It's too much to handle alone while simultaneously trying to make sure she doesn't do something stupid.

Like leave her fucking apartment when she was shot less than forty-eight hours ago.

This fucking woman...

My cock twitches, and I shake my head to try to clear the memory of how soft and sweet her lips were, even with all the pent-up tension and animosity between us. She kissed me like she wanted it. More, actually. Like she *needed it.*

And I had to force myself to move off her bed and settle in the chair across the room, or I would've done something that would've been very bad for both of us.

Even sitting across the room from her while she slept, keeping watch over her like some dark guardian angel, I couldn't quell the thoughts plaguing me.

Thoughts that were *not at all* angelic.

Far fucking from it.

They haven't dissipated in the day and a half since I left, when I have barely taken my eyes off her fucking front door except to get a new vehicle while I was sure she was asleep. I kept hoping she wouldn't leave. I fucking *prayed* to a God I don't believe in that she would stay put, give herself some time to recuperate.

But that woman is too damn stubborn to do that. She has to walk out onto the street like somebody didn't just try to kill her. Stumble out is more like it, actually. Her slow, deliberate steps prove she's not ready to be up and out, even if her life weren't in danger.

Yet, there she fucking is.

She makes it to the corner across from me and pauses at a red light, pressing her left hand into her side. I flinch and grit my teeth, practically experiencing the pain she must be in for myself.

Because I know what that feels like. Far too well. It's no fucking fun, no matter how tough you are or pretend to be. Pain is pain, and while it's absolutely possible to push through it when you need to, it hits you eventually.

Which means whatever got her up and out must be pretty fucking important. At least, it better be. Because now she's exposed to anyone who might want her hurt or worse.

Scanning every person on the street and passing cars, all I can see are potential threats. The problem is, half the fucking people visible look suspicious. People with shifty, angry eyes. People with hands in their pockets. People with phones to their ears who could be calling for a car to snatch her right off the street. The entire situation makes my shoulders tense.

A sketchy-looking guy with dark hair wearing a black peacoat steps up next to Viktoria. She glances over at him, her eyes drifting up his much taller frame. Her entire body tenses, and she takes a half-step away from him, closer to the curb.

He makes her nervous. That can't be good.

Vik is smart enough to sense danger. To know it when she sees it. She sure as hell did with me. And if she's getting a bad vibe off him, that likely means there's a reason—one we both should be wary of.

The light changes, and Vik allows the man to walk in front of her.

Smart move, Vik. Keep him in your line of sight. Don't let anyone you don't trust get your back.

She moves slowly to ensure she doesn't catch up to him, and once he hits my side of the street, the man turns to the right without looking back at her while something catches her eye to the left.

What has your attention, Vik?

Whatever it is, she turns her back to the man in order to cross the opposite corner. The glance he casts over his shoulder at her might not be caught by anyone else. It may not appear suspicious to anyone not watching for it. Nor would the twitch of his hand near his waist warrant concern for most people. But I can see it for exactly what it is.

"Fuck." I slip on the black balaclava sitting on my lap and jump from the van before I can talk myself out of it.

If I don't intervene now, Vik is likely to end up in the back of a dark SUV speeding away to her doom.

Her continued distraction with whatever is across the street allows me to slide up behind and clamp my hand over her mouth, silencing any cry for help while keeping a watch on the man behind us. Before he can react, I drag her toward the van, throw open the side door, and climb in with her.

True to form, Vik kicks and lashes out with her hands and feet as I slide the door shut behind us. Despite her physical protests and the scream she releases stinging my ears the moment I move my hand from her mouth, I manage to get the black fabric bag over her head and secure her wrists and ankles with zip ties that should hold her long enough to get where we're going. But then her feet connect with a very sensitive area of my body.

"*Fuck!*" I mutter a litany of other curses as I climb into the driver seat and take a quick survey of the area around us to ensure nobody saw what just went down.

But it's exactly what I anticipated. No one on the street saw it—too preoccupied with where they're going, or who they're talking to on their phones—or if they did, they don't give a shit. And the man who was watching her darted away, either disinterested or to alert whoever employed him that the target was just taken off the street by someone else.

I throw the van into drive and peel away from the curb, my cock and balls aching bad enough to make me want to throw up the cup of coffee that was my breakfast this morning.

Fucking woman...

Tearing off the mask and tossing it onto the seat beside me helps me suck in a few deep lungfuls of air, which somewhat quells the nausea. But Vik kicking and thrashing around as much as she can in the back tightens my chest again.

That woman can fight all she wants. She won't get out of those bindings, which is good for me because she'd probably try to gouge out my eyes and tear off what's left of my balls.

But there will be hell to pay when I get to where we're going.

8

VIKTORIA

L eft.

Right.

Sharp left.

Another left.

The familiar rumble of a train crossing the raised track above us.

This van the dickhead shoved me into speeds up, shifting me across the floor of the back.

Traffic whizzes by, then we slow.

Construction equipment.

Blaring horns and weaving that makes my stomach turn.

We've hit the BQE.

The sounds of the expressway overwhelm the air in the van for several minutes while I hold my breath, doing my damnedest to listen to every single noise.

A deeper form of darkness overtakes us for what feels like forever while the sound of the traffic around us changes. I tilt my head to angle my ear toward the wall of the van.

The Battery Tunnel. It has to be.

Even with this black cloth bag pulled over my head, preventing me from seeing anything about where we're going, that doesn't mean I can't gather as much information as possible with my other senses.

It might be essential to my escape when given the opportunity. I need to keep track of where we're heading. And as soon as the asshole who grabbed me tries to get me out of this piece-of-shit van, I'm going to make my move.

My body may be weak, but my will hasn't been affected by being shot by some soulless asshole. I will fight with whatever strength I have left to ensure this fucker doesn't get me somewhere I can't escape from. I've already let him move me from the location where he grabbed me, and I can't let it go further than that.

Who the hell does he think he is, anyway? Snatching me off the street in broad daylight. I'm a cop, for fuck's sake.

The entire NYPD is going to be looking for me. Maybe not until tomorrow since Hank already did his daily check-in with me today, but as soon as he can't get a hold of me in the morning, he's going to send every fucking officer in the Tri-State area on a manhunt.

And that creepy guy who crossed the street in front of me has to be connected. I don't get that *vibe* from just anyone. Only when I'm around someone who truly represents a threat.

He was probably sitting, watching my apartment this entire time, waiting for me to be stupid enough to step out onto the street where he could snatch me. And I played right into his hands. I got distracted when I saw Anya waiting for me at the restaurant and gave him my back even though I knew he was up to no good and was bad news.

It was fucking stupid and careless—something I'm going

to blame on the pain, the meds, and lack of good sleep the last few days. But I'm not going to make any more stupid mistakes, not when it could cost me my life.

The fact that whoever grabbed me didn't kill me right away means they need me *for* something or need something *from* me. That might buy me a little time to find a means of getting the fuck out of these bindings and away from that asshole.

Honking horns and the bustling sounds of Manhattan fill the van.

Stop.

Go.

Stop.

Go.

Lunchtime traffic can be a real killer, yet he headed straight into it.

Where the fuck is he taking me?

We inch through the streets, moving slowly while I wait for anything, like a noise or a smell, that will tell me exactly where we are. Manhattan for sure, but precisely where is less clear.

Then, the sound of the road under us changes again. Definitely a bridge.

Maybe the GW?

It definitely smells like the Hudson.

So, he's taking me to Jersey?

We come down off what I assume was the bridge, and the sound of the road beneath us changes again. He makes a hard right turn a little too fast, slamming me against the side of the van, sending a jolt of pain through my side. Grimacing, I try to push myself up, but it proves futile with my wrists bound.

After another couple of minutes pass, the van slows, and

the sound of metal grating against metal fills the air around me—almost like an industrial garage door opening.

Shit.

If he pulls the van inside somewhere, that eliminates any possibility of someone seeing me being dragged from the vehicle and coming to my rescue. But that's okay.

I'll fucking rescue myself.

This fucker is going to have to try to grab me, and even though my ankles are bound together, I still know how to aim for where I can do the most damage—his nuts.

If I connected with them earlier like I think I did, a second strike could do untold damage. And I'm more than ready to battle.

The van jerks to a stop, and I slide against the driver seat with an *umph.* If they're trying to keep me alive, this guy might want to drive a little bit more carefully. After being shot, the last thing I need is to be jostled around violently by a shitty driver.

A muffled grunt reaches my ears before the driver's side door opens and then slams closed, rocking the whole van.

I turn my head to place my ear toward the door.

No talking.

No sounds of people moving around.

Dead silence. So quiet, I can hear my own heart beating in my ears.

Wherever he brought me, we're alone.

Is that a good thing or a bad thing?

Probably a little bit of both. On the one hand, that means it will be a lot easier to take him out, but it also means his focus is likely one hundred percent on me. That could make my escape harder.

But there isn't any time to contemplate the situation further. The door slides open in front of me, and I tense, preparing myself for what I'm going to have to do if I want any chance of surviving this.

Watch out, fucker. Here I come.

REAPER

Every step I take around this van on my way to open the sliding door sends a zing of sizzling pain through my balls that's strong enough to make me fight back the need to wretch—again. And here I thought I had finally regained my faculties while making the drive from Vik's place in Brooklyn out to the safehouse in Jersey.

Vik got me good when she kicked out after I got her bound. If it weren't so agonizing, I might be able to admit how proud of her I am for fighting tooth and nail despite the fact that she's probably still hurting so badly from being shot.

Instead, I pause for a moment, my fingers curled in the handle of the door, and suck in a deep breath to prepare myself. She's going to come out kicking and screaming. There isn't a fucking doubt in my mind about that. But I don't want her to hurt herself trying to get away from me. That would defeat the entire purpose of this endeavor.

Rescue her only to hurt her more. That would be my fucking luck.

Patching her up once was more than enough for me. The memory of her bleeding in my arms has blended with other bloody ones to haunt even my waking hours. I don't need to go through that again, especially with her.

I tug open the door and barely have enough time to dodge to the left to avoid her bound feet flying out at me with all the force she can muster in her position on the floor.

Fucking knew it!

Pride wells in my chest as I wrap my arms around her thighs, and when she swings out to hit me with her hands fisted together, wrists bound in front of her, I swing her up over my shoulder like a sack of potatoes. I've carried men twice her size through IED-filled deserts dodging bullets. This, I can handle.

She releases a weak little squeal of protest, and I grit my teeth to bite back the need to apologize. That probably hurt, but it's far better than letting her do worse to herself.

"Knock it off." I smack the side of her thigh to emphasize my point.

She freezes instantly, shifting to twist her head toward the sound of my voice. "Dixon?"

Shit.

I hadn't intended for her to know I was the one who snatched her yet. Not until she had some time for the adrenaline to wear off a little bit so she could think more clearly. It was the only chance I had at getting her to see this situation without a red veil of anger coloring her view of it.

Well, she can speculate all she wants until I'm good and ready to reveal myself. Which isn't now. I stalk across the garage and into the freight elevator on the far side.

"Dixon, if that's you, I swear to God, I'm going to fucking kill you!"

Her shapely hips attempt to buck up, but she can barely budge with my arm wrapped firmly around her. Her hands connect with my lower back, but she doesn't have the angle to actually hurt me.

Thanks for the nice massage, sweetheart.

Biting back a snort of laughter, I reach up and jerk down

the metal door, securing us inside the elevator cab before jabbing my thumb into the button for the second floor where the converted loft living spaces are.

Old machinery cranks to life, groaning in protest. The high-pitched whine of the motor and grinding of gears fills the air, and she shifts on my shoulder violently, still trying to get the leverage she needs to inflict any damage on my back or push herself up from dangling upside down.

"Dixon, you better let me the fuck down right this moment."

I don't bother to hide my snort of laughter and tighten my grip around her thighs, making her struggling even more fruitless. The elevator car jerks to a stop, and I raise the cage and carry her, kicking and hitting, across the room to where one of the two bedrooms sits.

She isn't going to like this, but I'm doing it for her own good. The windowless room is only temporary digs until she's willing to acknowledge how much fucking danger she's really in and I can trust her not to do something stupid like try to leave.

If that ever happens...

Locating who shot at her while also tracking down where the girls are being held has proven beyond frustrating, and I can only hope the trajectory of this mission changes quickly.

Stopping in front of the bed, I give her legs another squeeze. "Stop fucking fighting, or you're going to hurt yourself."

I lean over and lower her onto the mattress, releasing her to bounce slightly across the surface toward the wall it's pushed against.

"I swear to God, I *am* going to kill you, Dixon."

She can sure try.

It's not like she'd be the first to try. Or even the hundredth. None of them succeeded, so I doubt the feisty, beautiful, and infuriating Detective Garin will have any better luck.

I reach out and tug at the top of the black fabric bag on her head, yanking it free and sending her dark hair out around her in a staticky, disheveled halo. Viktoria is anything *but* an angel, though. The fire that blazes in her green eyes might as well be the flames of Hell.

Only she thinks *I'm* the Devil.

She keeps her wrath-filled gaze on me while I slip my knife from my boot and cut the ties at her ankles and wrists, then step back before she can use her new-found freedom to her advantage.

Vik is going to have to face the reality that no matter how she might feel about me, I saved her damn life. She owes me a thank you—*another* one. But I'm going to give her some time to simmer down before I get into it with her.

I don't trust myself in here with her otherwise.

"Take some time to cool off. We'll talk later."

"You *kidnap* me and now you're leaving me in here?" She makes an attempt to leap off the bed, but I throw up a hand to stop her.

Thankfully, she complies; otherwise, I'm not sure where the fuck this would lead.

"It's for your own good. You'll thank me later. And stop calling me Dixon. It's Reaper."

9

VIKTORIA

P ale morning sunlight filters through the tiny crack under the door, the only real slice of freedom or the world that I can see.

If it's morning, that means he's had me locked up here for at least eighteen hours—maybe far more. Without a damn way out. I had planned to stay awake and jump him to attempt an escape when he opened the door again, but I must have dozed off because the plate with a sandwich and chips was sitting on the small nightstand beside the bed the next time I opened my eyes.

That bastard snuck in here, and I didn't even wake up.

I'd be a lot angrier with myself if I didn't know how stealthy and well-trained he is or how badly my body needed the rest. It's not like trying to attack Reaper to get out of here would have worked, anyway. He would have made sure of that—all those skills focused on keeping me locked up instead of against our common enemy.

And other than getting up to use the small bathroom

attached to the room, I haven't moved off this bed, the exhaustion of fighting against my "attacker" making me so tired, it felt like I had taken a step back in my recovery rather than one forward.

All because of fucking Dixon...Reaper...whatever the hell I'm supposed to call him.

First, he terrified me by breaking into my apartment. Then, he patched me up and kissed me until I could barely breathe. And now, he's kidnapped me and thrown me in this room like he somehow owns me.

Fucking jerkface.

A shadow blocks the light, the knob turns, and Reaper pushes open the door and steps inside the room, closing it behind him with a finality that sends a chill down my spine at the same time it brings a heated fury raging through my blood.

He stops a few steps back from the bed, arms crossed over his chest in his signature stance. "Are you ready to have a calm, rational conversation about this, or do you need a little more time to cool off?"

Calm, rational conversation?

"Are you fucking serious right now? You *kidnapped* me!"

He points a finger at me, his eyebrows raised. "Hey, I did it to save your ass."

"That doesn't make it any less illegal, asshole."

"Now, that's just splitting hairs. Would you rather I had let that creep on the street nab you and then wait around for a ransom call or to find your body in the Hudson?"

I scowl at him even though it doesn't seem to impede anything he does.

He watches me with icy, hard eyes. "You could say thank you. It would be a lot easier than arguing with me."

Leaning back against the wall the small bed is pushed

against, I fist my hands so tightly at my sides that my nails dig painfully into my palms. Flashes of the man in the peacoat and the unease that crept over me take over my mind.

I had assumed he was the one who nabbed me, and while, in reality, it was Reaper, it could just as easily have been that man...or anyone else, for that matter. "You can't know he was going to grab me."

Reaper barks out a laugh and shakes his head. "Yes, I can. After you passed out the other night, do you know what I did?"

Heat spreads up my neck and over my face at the memory of the kiss. The way his lips moved fluidly against mine. His warm palms cupping my cheeks. That smug smile tilting his lips when he told me he wouldn't quit.

I shift uncomfortably on the bed under his assessment —the way his eyes bore into me like he can see I'm reliving that moment and the way my body is reacting to that. "I know you stayed for a while."

He nods slowly. "And you were so out of it that you didn't even notice that I nailed your goddamn window shut."

"You what?"

His nostrils flare, his jaw clenching. "Vik, it was so easy to get into your place, a child could have fucking done it. So, after I made sure no one else was getting in, I secured a new vehicle, came back, and sat and watched your place for the next day and a half."

"They have a term for that, you know..." I raise an eyebrow at him. "Stalker."

He snorts and shakes his head again, that cocky grin turning up the corner of his lips. "I was thinking *hero*."

Scoffing, I roll my eyes. "You would."

Annoyance tightens his shoulders, the muscles bunching like he's trying desperately to contain his desire to lash out at me. "You want to know what I saw during those almost two days, Vik?"

"A lot of angry New Yorkers?"

"Well, yeah, that, but I also saw a dark SUV sitting across from your place for hours on end. Then a new vehicle would show up and they'd switch places. Almost like they were doing shifts. You want to know what that was?"

I scowl and give him my best glower. "I'm not an idiot, Reaper. I'm a damn cop. It was obviously surveillance."

"Right. Probably the same fuckers who shot at you. Probably connected to the guy in the black coat who was going to nab you off the street before I did." He inhales a deep breath like he's trying to steady his nerves; though, what he has to be nervous about remains elusive. "He was watching you from the second you stepped onto the sidewalk, Vik. He only went the opposite direction once you crossed the street to let you get in front of him. He had turned his attention back to you as soon as you got distracted by whatever you saw across the street."

Anya.

"My sister...I was supposed to meet her for lunch. She's going to be looking for me."

He reaches into his back pocket, pulls out my cell phone, and jiggles it back and forth in his hand. "Oh, I've already had a lovely chat with your sister."

"You *what*?"

"I saw the multiple text messages from her wondering where you were after you didn't show up for lunch, so I texted her back, pretended to be you, and told her you were hung up with something at work." He raises a dark eyebrow.

"Interestingly enough, she asked if it was about what she got you the information on. Me...I'm assuming?"

Shit.

He shrugs nonchalantly. "I told her it was nothing to worry about and I would be in touch with her in a few days. She told you to be careful."

Dammit.

Sometimes, we'll go weeks without talking to each other, so she won't suspect anything not hearing from me for a while, especially if he told her I was working on something. It's not unusual for me to go deep into a case, shut out the entire world for a while.

But she isn't the only one in my life.

"What about Hank? He's going to be looking for me. So is the precinct."

Reaper grins. "Hank, I can handle." He crosses the room and holds out my phone to me. "The department...you're going to."

"Like hell I am."

He squats down to face level with me, his eyes hard and determined as he holds up the phone and shakes it in front of me. "You're going to call them and tell them that you're sicker than you thought and that you're going to take two weeks off since you have so much built-up vacation to ensure that you are one hundred percent before you come back."

"Fuck you, Reaper. No way. You're not keeping me locked up here for two weeks."

"Didn't say I was. Just until we get this sorted out. But I want to make sure I bought us enough time, just in case." He reaches out and wraps his free hand around my wrist, turns up my palm, and sets the phone in it. "Make the call."

Where his palm connects with my skin practically

sizzles with electricity that travels up my arm, over my chest, and straight down between my legs.

What would those calloused palms and fingertips feel like in other places?

I lick my lips and glance at his involuntarily.

"Viktoria..."

Crap.

I let my gaze meet his again.

"Make. The. Call. I can't be spending my time ensuring your safety and do what I need to do to locate the girls and get *them* to safety. I can't be constantly worrying about someone dragging you off the street or breaking your fucking windowpane to get in. I can't be wondering if you're collapsed and bleeding on the damn floor of your apartment."

"Shit, Reaper." I plaster on a saccharine sweet and fake smile. "It almost sounds like you care."

Silence hangs between us for a second, his hand never moving from around my wrist. I meant it as a joke. A jab at the fact that he's so stony and impossible. But he seems to have taken it literally, and it appears to be making him very uneasy. He squeezes my wrist gently, then swallows thickly and shakes his head.

"Shit. I do, Vik. That's the fucking problem." He releases me, pushes to his feet, and points to the phone. "Make the call."

I scowl at him but dial the number for the precinct despite my anger and reluctance and confusion over what just happened between us. While I may not agree with his tactics, he has a point. If what he says is true and people have been watching me, waiting for an opportunity to strike, it's quite possible that man on the street today was one of them and that they're connected to the shooting.

And I can't only think about my own anger and animosity toward the situation—and the man who put me in it—right now. Not when there are potentially dozens of innocent girls somewhere in the city who need the help that only someone like Reaper can provide.

It would be selfish of me not to do this.

The man I need to talk to answers on the third ring. "Captain Miller."

"Hey, it's Vik. I'm going to need two weeks off..."

REAPER

Vik ends the call with her boss and jabs her finger into the phone with so much aggression, I'm surprised the screen doesn't crack. I step forward and hold out my hand for the phone.

Her jaw drops incredulously, her green eyes darkening with her anger. "Seriously?"

I raise an eyebrow. "You think I'm going to let you keep your phone? How dumb do I look?"

"Dumb enough to think that you could keep me locked up here and that I would just comply."

Like I ever fucking thought it would be easy.

With a sigh, I snatch the phone out of her hand with a little too much force. "We have to figure out who wants you dead and why. The faster we can do that, the sooner I can let you go." I slip the phone back into my pocket. "Did you recognize the guy in the black coat?"

Vik closes her eyes for a second, likely running through the events of yesterday in her head. "No." She opens her eyes and shakes her head. "I didn't. But that doesn't mean anything. I've arrested a lot of shitheads, any number of whom could want revenge."

"Anyone in particular with a vendetta against you? Someone whose sentence may have just been completed and they got released? Someone you sent upriver who has an angry family?"

She shakes her head again and pulls up her knees against her chest with a little wince. "Not that I can think of off the top of my head."

"Which makes me think this is connected to B66."

Her brown furrows. "What makes you say that?"

I pace the small room, running through what we do know in my head. "Because someone had enough manpower and resources to have a car sitting on you for two days in shifts. Who else would spend that kind of money and time?"

"True. And while the guy wasn't familiar, that doesn't mean he isn't one of Yankovich's minions. His network is huge and spreads out across New York and the surrounding boroughs, so he's bound to have hundreds if not thousands of foot soldiers I've never seen. Which is probably why they used him specifically. So that I wouldn't suspect anything."

"But what I don't get is...why would the Russians want you dead?"

Her eyes widen slightly. "Shit..."

That doesn't sound good at all.

"What is it?"

She chews on her bottom lip, her eyes meeting mine with a mild hint of panic in their depths. "Nothing. Never mind. Just being paranoid."

"No, you're not, Vik. I have to know *everything* if we want to figure out *anything*."

With a long sigh, she drops her head and runs her hands

back through her long, dark hair, squeezing her eyes closed. "I guess it's possible I was recognized at B66."

I freeze mid-step and turn to fully face her. "What the fuck do you mean *recognized*?"

Vik slowly lifts her head and opens her eyes. "I grew up with those people, Reaper. Not Yankovich specifically but his type. And everyone knew his family. I'm from Brighton Beach. I became a cop so that I wouldn't get sucked into that life the way so many of the girls who were working at the club have been. But a lot of my friends didn't get out and ended up in places like that. People I haven't seen or talked to in over a decade, maybe more. I guess it's possible..."

Fuck.

I sigh, rubbing at the tension building in the back of my neck. "It's possible someone you grew up with still recognized you when you were there with Hank."

She shrugs slightly. "It hadn't occurred to me when he asked me to go. I thought I was far enough removed—physically as well as in time—that no one would identify me, or it wouldn't cause a problem if they did."

"But if someone *did* recognize you, and they knew you became a cop...then they would also know you weren't at B66 to enjoy the nightlife and were likely snooping around and that you might cause a problem for whatever is about to go down."

Her lip disappears under her teeth again, and she nods. "It's a definite possibility."

"Shit." I shove my hands through my hair. "That would explain them coming after you specifically. Maybe they didn't make Hank out as a cop and just thought he was a boyfriend or someone you dragged along as cover. It makes sense *you'd* be the target. The one they for *sure* knew was a threat to their business."

"Oh, God..." She sucks in a breath and presses her hand to her side. "It's my fault I got shot." Her panic-filled gaze meets mine. "That *you* got shot."

Oh, hell...

This looks like the beginnings of a full-on panic attack.

I drop onto the bed next to her and push her hair back from her face, tangling my fingers in the soft tresses I have no right to be touching. "Don't do that, Vik. I'm fine. Just another scar to add to dozens of other ones. And you will be fine soon enough."

She doesn't respond to my words, just watches me with unshed tears shimmering in her eyes.

"Do you see now why you need to stay here? Why you need to stay hidden?"

"No." Indignation flashes in her gaze. "I caused this. I need to be out there helping you, doing what I can. I need to get my feet on the pavement to help locate what we need to save the girls even more now."

Christ, this woman is stubborn.

I shake my head and tighten my hold in her hair, forcing her face to angle up to mine. "You might be the most frustrating woman I've ever met."

The corner of her mouth twitches, like she's fighting a smile or potentially the desire to slap me. "I could say the same for you."

Despite knowing how dangerous it is, I can't fight the smirk that pulls at my lips. "That I'm the most frustrating woman you've ever met?"

That earns me the tiniest crack of a grin from her. "You drive me fucking crazy. You know that?"

I nod slowly. "I sure as hell do, Vik. The feeling is more than mutual."

"And you're not going to let me out of here, are you?"

Shaking my head, I lean in closer until my lips barely brush against hers. "Not until I know you're safe."

Her hands come to my chest, but rather than push me away, she curls her fingers into the fabric of my shirt, using it to drag me tightly against her. "And what if I fight my way out?"

A low chuckle rumbles in my chest, pressing it harder against her ample breasts. "I'd have to tie you up."

Her heart thunders against mine, her breath coming hot and fast. "Don't threaten me with a good time, Reaper."

Fucking hell.

I tug her hair harder, tightening my grip to a point that must be painful for her. A warning I hope she understands before she pushes this any further. "You wouldn't survive a good time with me, sweetheart."

10

VIKTORIA

Reaper's lips crash down on mine so fast, it steals my retort and my breath, along with any ability to continue to fight the draw I feel toward this man who's all kinds of wrong for me.

Just yesterday, this killer, this criminal willing to take a life rather than allow me to do my job, literally kidnapped me. Yet, for some reason I can't even begin to understand, I trust that he would never hurt me. At least, not intentionally.

And the way his touch ignites the tiniest fibers of my being, all I can think about is how damn good it's going to feel to have his rough hands work over every inch of me.

Slowly. Softly. Brutally.

It won't matter. I'll take it all.

Anything and everything he has to give me.

Reaper doesn't disappoint. He wraps one of his arms around my waist and squeezes firmly to drag me up to straddle his lap, careful not to touch my other side. Even if he did, any pain I'm feeling is so easily pushed back behind the need overtaking my entire being.

Our lips wage the same battle we've been having verbally since the moment we met, while our tongues dance in a duel for supremacy. But neither one of us is going to win this one. Neither of us will give in or give up power. If anything, he's made that even more clear since he brought me here. He sees it as his responsibility to keep me safe and save those girls, and mine is to those girls, too, but also to the law and to ensure its upheld for everyone living in the city.

None of that matters at this moment. Not in this tiny, windowless room—wherever the hell we might be in fucking Jersey. All that does is the brush of his calloused fingertips up my spine and the roll of my hips to grind down against his hard cock between us in just the right spot.

A tiny whimper falls from my lips and into his mouth, and he sucks it down greedily, shifting his hands to the hem of my shirt and tugging up until I reluctantly pull back enough to let him move it. I release my death grip on the fabric of his tee, and he drags mine up and off, letting it fall to the floor beside the bed.

His blue eyes, darkened to almost navy by his lust, focus on the red blush spreading over my chest. This isn't the first time he's seen me like this—with nothing but a thin layer of lacy fabric covering my breasts—but somehow, it feels like I'm exposed more now than I was the other night when I was perhaps at my weakest. Now, it seems almost like his heated gaze blazes right through what little physically separates us and past the skin that should protect me, like he's burrowing his way deep to expose everything I try so hard to hide.

My need to prove myself.

My desire to win.

The pulsating need I feel for him.

He reaches out a hand and pulls the fabric of my bra down, exposing my nipple to the chilly air of the room. Rough fingertips twist it, sending a jolt straight to my core and making it clench in anticipation.

Fumbling between us, I manage to find the hem of his T-shirt while he releases my aching breast and undoes his belt. I tug up at the soft cotton, and he lets me pull it over his broad shoulders and head. The black fabric falls to the bed beside me, but my focus is on what's directly in front of me.

Rock-solid muscle.

Sun-bronzed skin marred by too many red, angry, puckered scars to count.

But Reaper doesn't give me a chance to consider them long because he flips me onto my back and kneels between my legs, pulls off his belt, and jerks down his pants, letting his thick, hard cock spring free.

I swallow thickly and dart out my tongue to wet my suddenly dry lips.

His fingertips tickle the sensitive skin along the edge of the waistband of my yoga pants. Back and forth. Back and forth. Sending flutters of anticipation through my body and building the heat growing between my legs.

The pressure there urges me to arch my hips, seeking some sort of friction, some sort of release, and almost as if he knows what I need, he slides his hand down and drags his thumb up the seam of the stretchy black fabric to my clit. My pussy immediately spasms in response, and I drop my head back and squeeze my eyes closed against the flutter of need growing from that very spot.

"Fuck…" The word tumbles from my mouth, and I clutch the bedspread beneath me in my fists. But instead of urging him to move us to where we both want to be, my distress seems to only make him more determined to torture me.

Oh, great. Kidnapping and torture.

One side of his lips turns up smugly, and he rolls his thumb there, languidly, so damn slowly that he's ensuring I feel every tiny brush, every little change in pressure, making me squirm under his touch. I force open my eyes again just in time to see him take his cock in his other hand and stroke it, never taking his crystal-blue gaze off me.

At least this isn't just torment for me. The white-knuckle grip Reaper has on his erection as he draws his palm along his length and the tense, coiled muscles in his arms and chest tell me he's just as on-edge as I am.

Yet, he seems intent on dragging this out, brushing his thumb over my clit and swirling it slowly until I can feel how soaked the fabric between my legs is. Embarrassingly wet, really. The kind of wet virgins get when they're touched this way for the first time, not how a grown-ass woman who has had her fair share of lovers does when she's looked at the right way by the wrong man.

If he doesn't tear these pants off me soon, I might spontaneously combust...

I release my death-grip on the bedspread and move my hands to the top of my pants, curling my fingers under the edge of the material.

If that doesn't give him the hint, then nothing will.

With a grin playing on his lips, he releases his hold on his dick and shifts his hand from between my legs to grasp my waistband and peel the fabric, along with my thong, down my legs and off my feet, letting it fall unceremoniously into a pile on the floor.

His darkening eyes flicker straight between my legs,

zeroing in on the spot I want him so badly. Desire blazes in his gaze, only eclipsed by the anger still lingering at me or at the situation, the same anger I keep pushing deep down so I can get what I want without second-guessing it.

He leans forward and brushes his left hand against the bandage on my skin while he glides the other up between my thighs and slips a finger inside me.

"Oh, God."

His hand at my side presses there firmly, and it almost numbs the lingering pain, or maybe it's the way his finger moves inside me then pulls out as he swirls his thumb around my clit that makes euphoria the only feeling I can manage to process even though a million are raging within me right now.

Propping himself on his elbow, he kicks his jeans free while he continues to work me over with his hand, forcing me even deeper into becoming a needy, quivering mass. With his eyes locked on mine, he asks me a million questions without ever voicing one, and I answer with a single look.

He kisses up my neck until his warm lips brush against my ear. "Tell me if I'm hurting you."

I manage a groan of response and a slight nod before he pulls his hand from between my legs and pushes his cock into me so fast, there's barely any time to prepare myself. "Fuck, Reaper!"

Not that I could have ever prepared myself for this man.

I never saw him coming.

And I never stood a chance...

REAPER

Fuuuuuuuuuuuuucccccccccccccccckkkkkkkkkkkkkkkkkkk!

Vik clenches her pussy tighter around my cock, wraps one hand around my neck, and digs the nails of her other hand into my bare chest. The move only urges me to push in even deeper until I bottom out inside her and capture her surprised gasp with my lips.

She groans against my mouth, clasping my flesh inside her as I draw back my hips and slam in again. Her hot breath rushes out, and I drink it in the same way she does mine with each pant.

Despite her injury—or maybe *in spite* of it—she doesn't tell me to stop. To go slower. To be gentler. To take my time with her. That isn't what she wants.

This isn't making love. I haven't done that in so long that I'm not even sure I remember what that feels like anymore. But this isn't *that.* This is hard and demanding. This is fucking away the tension we've felt every time we've been in the same room together. This is both of us proving a point. That I'm in control here but she's never going to back down from me or any challenge. Neither of us is willing to break, both determined to come out on top.

I complete every mission—including this one. And right now, making her come is at the top of my priority list. I find a rhythm and angle that has the head of my cock dragging against that perfect spot inside her. Her nails score the skin on my chest and the back of my neck, and I roll my hips, grinding my pelvic bone down against her clit with each thrust.

Her lips fall away from mine, and she drops her head back, exposing her long neck, dark hair spread out around her on the pillow. "Oh...fuck..." She wraps her left leg around my hip and digs her heel into my lower back. "Right there. Fuck! Just like that."

There isn't any hiding the deep rumble of satisfaction in my chest when it's pressed to hers. Vik writhes under me, her hips meeting mine fluidly, like we're meant to move and fit together this way. And she's wound tight. So damn tight. That was my intent with the way I teased her earlier. I had to get her ready and primed well because I knew once I was inside her that there was absolutely no way in *hell* I would last long enough to do her properly.

Not when it's been this long.

Not when it's *this* woman.

Her anger. Her touch. Her righteous indignation and unwavering defiance. It's all so beautiful and toxic at the same time. The perfect mix to create an epic explosion now that we've finally come together like this.

And every thrust of my cock inside her wet, welcome heat drives me closer to losing control, to taking this beyond what she can handle after what she just went through.

She shifts her hand down my neck, over my shoulder, to my back, her fingertips brushing over the jagged scars there —reminders of the last things I want to be thinking of while like this with Vik. It drives me into her with a renewed force and determination to push us both to the brink of insanity.

A familiar, warm haze encroaches on the edges of my vision, making Vik's face come in and out of focus, and I take her mouth with mine again in a vicious, bruising kiss.

"Come for me, Vik." I grit my teeth, the muscles in my neck and jaw straining with my effort to hold back what my body demands. "Fucking come!"

Vik hates anyone telling her what to do or how to live her life. She's proven over and over again that she needs to be the one in control, but the moment that final word leaves my lips, her entire body seizes like something otherworldly takes hold of her.

She gasps and clutches at my back and neck, pulling me even closer while I pound into her rippling cunt. Every drive in, her body tries to keep me there, and it fights me on each withdrawal.

It doesn't take long—only a few more thrusts—for the tsunami I've been holding back finally crashes over me. The pleasure and pain. The truths of where we are and what we've done to get here. It all threatens to drown me in her wildly bucking hips until I finally empty myself inside her and she collapses beneath me, her hands falling away from my warm, sweaty skin.

Jesus...what the hell was that?

I roll to her right side, putting myself between her and the door, and drop my arm over my eyes. No matter what just happened between us, I don't trust her. This woman wouldn't think twice about using this as an opportunity to sneak away from her "cell."

My chest heaving, my breaths coming out in hard pants, I do my best to slow them down, to regain control over my body and my mind. Because I clearly just lost it. Giving in to whatever the hell this is with Vik makes this all so much harder. So much more complicated. It makes what I'm going to have to do hurt more than it ever should. More than I should ever *let* it.

Vik shifts next to me and rolls onto her side, lifting her hand to drag her fingers over the still-fresh wound on my arm and the scars on my chest and side. Her featherlight, almost reverent, touch sends a chill of dread through me that I haven't felt in a really fucking long time.

I shift away and sit on the edge of the bed, running my hands back through my hair, squeezing at the tension in the back of my neck and shoulders that suddenly feels like it's about to snap me in half.

It should have been an obvious move to tell her to leave me alone, to back the fuck off if she knows what's good for her. I should have known this woman *never* cares about what's good for her.

That soft touch flutters over the scars on my back. Slowly. One by one. It takes far longer than it should for anyone still breathing to get through them all. Sometimes, it surprises me that I still am. Often, I wonder why I, of all people, survived what I have when so many men more worthy of living died so tragically.

It's why I avoid situations like this. When people will ask questions I don't want to answer. When they'll make assumptions about my wounds and how I "earned" these scars. When they'll look at me like I'm a hero when all I feel like is a fucking fraud most days. The "lucky" one who got away relatively unscathed when those better than me fell.

I push to my feet to escape her touch and avoid looking back while I grab my clothes from the floor. But I don't *have* to look to know she's watching me...and being uncharacteristically quiet for Vik. It's in her cop nature to ask questions, to want to know someone's background and what makes them tick. It's how she gets into the heads of the people she interrogates. She reads them like open books and plays them until they fold in her favor.

But that won't happen with me.

If she hasn't learned that by now, she's going to at this moment.

I jerk on my jeans but don't bother buttoning them before I head for the door.

"Where are you going?" Her question holds every bit of incredulousness I would expect her to have after that.

"To have a fucking smoke and make some calls."

"And you're just leaving me here?"

I suck in a deep breath, keeping my back to her as I open the door. "It's where you belong..."

My foot crosses the threshold out into the loft, but I pause and turn back, finally letting my gaze land on her. Spread out across the small bed, propped up on her elbow, naked and practically glowing with my fucking cum still inside her, Vik locks her hard eyes with mine, waiting for me to say the words she knows are coming.

"Since you clearly can't be trusted not to get into trouble. Even in here."

11

VIKTORIA

The scalding-hot water in the tight shower in the minuscule bathroom attached to my "cell" can't warm me from the freeze that settled over me when Reaper's icy gaze fell on me from the doorway.

He had shut down completely. Any connection we made in that bed ended the moment I touched his scars. It was like flipping a switch. And now that I've seen a glimpse of why they call him Reaper, I don't know if I can ever shake this chill.

Because I saw it in those blue depths. The detachment. That is what allows him to do it. That is the man who can so easily say he'll wipe out anyone involved with this trafficking ring rather than let the law handle them. The man willing to spill so much blood and have it on his own hands.

Another shiver rolls down my spine, and I reach out and crank the water even hotter until it stings, pelting my hypersensitive skin.

I knew it was there. Knew what I was getting myself into

when I agreed to be involved with this mission instead of running it up the food chain like I should have. But I let Hank and Reaper convince me to go along with it, anyway. Knowing it went against everything I believe in and fought for my entire life.

Shit. What the hell am I doing?

I slam my palm against the old mint-green tile, my frustration boiling over again.

This entire situation is just...unbelievable. I never could have anticipated it would lead to this—being locked up in a room by a man I can't stand and can't seem to control myself around at the same time under some misguided plan to protect me.

Maybe it was stupid to think no one would recognize me at B66, but I left that life behind so long ago, went to community college, then got my job with the Department as soon as I graduated, and never looked back, never even set foot in Brighton Beach again to ensure I made a clean break from everyone associated with that life. It hurt Mom and Dad while they were alive that they always had to come to see me rather than me go to them...but they also understood it. Because it was what they wanted for me, too, ultimately. To get out. To have all the success in the world they never did, no matter how hard they worked.

But now, I've been sucked back into the world, and while Hank and Reaper and the Satan's Knights might be arguing that this is all for the greater good, that part of me that's always strived to not become those people I fight so hard against, those who don't respect or abide by the law, doesn't want to fully accept that. *Can't* accept that.

My chest tightens uncomfortably just thinking about what's coming in the near future, and I turn and drop my head forward, letting the water hit the back of my neck.

Reaper may be right about his having to watch and protect me being a distraction from our greater focus, but it doesn't mean he needs to keep me locked up here and away from being involved with the search and rescuing of those girls.

I have to be.

If I let them fully cut me out of this, it won't be possible for me to intervene before things are taken too far, before I can steer them in the lawful direction. Because there's still hope at this point. There's still a *chance* there might be a way to do this without breaking every code I live by and every societal rule I stand for.

But maybe that's just wishful thinking on my part. Because those codes didn't seem to mean anything a few moments ago when Reaper was inside me. They didn't seem to mean much when I was urging him to keep going and relishing every movement under his hard, tight body.

So, perhaps I'm a fraud. Perhaps I am too far gone to bring us back from this dark path we've started down. Because what we just did changes everything, whether or not we try to deny and attempt not to let it.

Reaper said it himself—I even get into trouble in this room.

And he's the kind of trouble I don't need, the kind of trouble that leaves a permanent mark—maybe not visibly like the scars that mar his body, but on your soul, one you feel for a lifetime burning there, searing and reminding you of your mistake.

And since the water is doing nothing to make me feel better, I turn it off and step out onto the cracked tile floor, wrapping myself in the towel hanging from a hook on the wall. Another shiver runs down my spine despite the heavy, warm air, and I reach up and wipe the fog from the cheap, dingy mirror.

What the hell are you doing, Viktoria?

A complete stranger stares back at me with cloudy, tired, green eyes. So much has happened in the last week, so much that I never thought could. So much that has changed everything.

My partner lied to me and betrayed my trust. I was involved in an off-books investigation and shooting I kept a secret from the police department. And ultimately, I agreed to help a group of vigilantes take down an organization that should be dealt with through the proper channels.

The Viktoria who looks back at me isn't the one I thought she was. She never would've ended up in bed with Reaper. Yet, my entire body still tingles, remembering his touch, and my pussy clenches at the memory of what he felt like thrusting into me with such force, such aggression and passion. It's hard to say I don't want to be that girl, the one who could just let go and take what she wanted for once without thinking about the consequences far off in the future.

But I don't think my conscience will let me do that. Thinking about it alone weighs so heavily on my chest that I can barely take a breath.

I have to look for an opening—a way to get what is about to go down into the hands of the FBI or the Department, someone who can control it and ensure no innocent bystanders—or Hank or Reaper—get hurt or worse.

They might have the best of intentions. That's one thing I don't question about Reaper. That man believes whole-heartedly that what he's doing is right. The problem is he won't draw any lines and is willing to go to any lengths, and it's just not something I can let happen. Even if Reaper admitted he *does* care about me in *some* way. It's not enough to give up everything I've ever stood for.

REAPER

Another deep, long inhale off my cigarette sends nicotine coursing through my system. It's exactly what I needed and yet not nearly enough to calm the anxiety building inside me. I flick the lighter open and closed, the familiar rhythmic clicking sound doing little to soothe me the way it normally does.

And it isn't just about what just happened between Viktoria and me; it's knowing what will happen as soon as we get the information we need to locate the girls.

Mouth and Chaos should be here in a matter of days, and by then, either Hank or the MC or I will hopefully have the information we need to take immediate action. I trust my brothers with my life, but doing something like this on American soil is a lot different than anything we've done before. It holds a lot more risk, much deeper ramifications if we get caught.

I'm not afraid to face those because I know what I'm doing is right, and I can handle anything anyone can throw at me. But Viktoria is another matter.

She has ideals. Ones that can never withstand what she'll need to do if she's involved with this or with me. What just happened between us can't happen again. Not if we want to maintain focus and be able to walk away from this unattached and her still holding her job.

And that's the only option.

Because when all this is finally over, she'll be back to

being a pit bull detective hunting down New York's worst scum, and I'll do what I do best—disappear somewhere I can live my life on my own terms without having to answer to anyone anymore. That ended when Uncle Sam said I could no longer do my job properly. And honestly, the way things were six months ago, they were probably right.

Keeping her locked in there is the only way to ensure she doesn't get in too deep. When we finally get the location and move on it, Vik won't be there. I can't expose her to that kind of danger—to herself or her career.

Not after I already did that in her bed.

Being with me is the most dangerous thing she's ever done.

I drop the cigarette onto the grates of the fire escape and grind it out with my boot as I slip the lighter back into my pocket. The sounds of the street below fill the air, and I'm tempted to remain out here to avoid the tension of what's inside. But I can't ignore the reality forever, no matter how much I'd love to.

There is work to be done.

Dirty work.

Things are about to get bloody.

I step inside the loft, and my back pocket buzzes.

Fuck.

That better be someone with some good news because anything else will only stretch my already-thin control to its breaking point. What happened with Viktoria was only the tip of the iceberg, a brief, small glimpse of what I'm capable of when I'm unleashed.

I pull out my phone, but the screen is black. "Shit."

It must be Viktoria's.

The deception with her sister may have worked in texts, but if she's calling now, Viktoria isn't likely to cooperate and get on the line. Not after I just walked out and locked her back in there.

My pocket buzzes again, and I grab Vik's phone and glance at the screen to find a flurry of text messages from Hank asking if she's okay that started hours ago.

Fuck.

While we were getting busy in there, he's been trying to get a hold of her and can't, so he's panicking.

Really, Vik? Two fucking weeks?

What the fuck is going on?

Come on, answer me goddamnit.

Text me.

Call me.

If I don't fucking hear from you in one minute, I'm coming over.

Shit!

That was almost an hour ago. Which means Hank may already be at her place, or at the very least, on his way there.

Almost as if on cue, her phone dings with a notification from her video doorbell. I press the button for the camera and find Hank banging on the door like a fucking madman.

Fuck. This is just what I don't need right now.

He's liable to start a manhunt for her if I don't intervene—and do it fast. I scroll through her contacts to find his name and hit send before bringing the phone to my ear.

Hank answers on the first ring. "Vik? Where the hell are

you? I've been texting you and calling you. I'm in front of your place."

"It isn't Vik. It's Reaper."

"Dixon? Why the hell do you have Vik's phone? I think Vik is missing. She's not answering my texts or taking my calls. I'm outside of her apartment—"

I scrub my hand over my face and sigh. "She's fine. I have her."

"You *have* her? What does that even mean?"

"It means that she's safe and you don't need to worry about her."

"The hell I don't." Hank's indignation comes through the phone loud and clear, and I can't say I blame him for it. "I don't know what the fuck you're doing, Dixon, but I don't fucking like it. Put her on the damn phone. Now."

I settle onto one of the stools at the kitchen counter. "Now isn't a good time. But trust me when I say this was necessary. I saw a car surveilling her place."

""Back up. Why the hell were *you* surveilling her place?"

"That doesn't matter. She left to meet her sister for lunch and I noticed someone was following her. He looked suspicious as fuck—"

"Hold on. She left to meet her sister?" The fucker just cut me off, but his response tells me we're on the same page about how stupid it was of her to be leaving so soon after being shot. "Never mind. That's irrelevant. Continue. What happened?"

"I had to intervene. I grabbed her."

"Is she okay?"

The vivid memory of her screaming my name while I pounded into her flashes through my head, stirring my cock. "Yep. A little pissed off by what I had to do, but she'll get over it. I couldn't put her at risk like that."

She's already put herself at risk by going to B66 in the first place, thinking no one would recognize her. It was reckless and stupid. She could have gotten herself killed.

Why do I care so damn much?

The only way I've survived this long is by never allowing myself to care about a woman. I couldn't and continue to do what I did. Couldn't be away for weeks or months at a time, knowing she would worry and be miserable. Couldn't leave behind a widow when I inevitably didn't come home.

This is no different. I can't let her get under my skin anymore. It isn't good for either of us.

Hank blows out a long breath. "So, with you being preoccupied with Vik, I guess you don't have anything new on Yankovich."

"Nothing worth mentioning."

"Well, I may have made a dent. Long story short, Parrish gave me a tip, and I checked it out. Michail has a place in Williamsburg where he's keeping Vlad's wife, Anastasia, and her two kids. I followed her for a couple of days and made contact. First at a coffee shop she visits regularly, then when that proved to be a bust, Parrish and I cornered her at her kid's school. It was the only way to get close without her guards. We tried talking some sense into her, but the woman is stubborn as shit and dead set on protecting her brother-in-law. If we can get her to flip, she might clear the path to Michail, or at the very least, lead us in the right direction."

It's a good lead, one that definitely has potential. "You think she might know where he's keeping the girls or holding the auction?"

"I'm not sure, but she knew who I was and was pissed. Made me think that she knows something."

"Well, now that I know Vik is safe, I can get back to pounding the pavement and talking to my contacts to see what I can find out." And hopefully, they'll be more forth-coming once I have more firepower here. "I have two buddies coming into town to help. They should be here soon. Then, hopefully, we can plan our next move more easily."

"And what about Vik? Do we know who the guy sniffing around her was?"

I glance at the closed and locked door keeping her contained. "I'm pretty sure it was one of Yankovich's guys and that they were who took a shot at her the other night, too."

"Fuck. Why her though? Why not me or the Satan's Knights?"

"She said she might have been recognized at B66. Did you know she grew up in Brighton Beach?"

"Well, yeah, but to my understanding she hasn't been back there since before college. So let me get this straight, she thinks someone from her old neighborhood placed her at the club, told Yankovich, and he sent someone to silence her. Should we be worried?" "I'll handle Vik."

"I've known her a lot longer than you, Dixon, and fair warning—it's a lot harder than you think."

"Trust me," I growl, "I'm more than aware of how hard she is to handle."

I end the call and shove the phone back into my pocket, my gaze automatically darting back to the locked door across the open loft space.

I'm not in any position to be trying to deal with her again right now. She needs more time to cool off, and I need time to figure out my next move without her in my orbit, fucking with my head and my ability to think clearly.

It's time to get out and see what I can shake loose.

12

REAPER

The blood pooling at my feet should probably concern me. It should be pushing me into action, to move, to step out of it, to do *something*, but instead, all I can think about is how peaceful Vik looked when I opened the door to her room to leave food for her before I left earlier.

Either she was passed out, or she's one hell of a good fake sleeper. Either way, her chest rose and fell in that steady rhythm, the fabric of the T-shirt she slipped on after we fucked unable to conceal her nipples straining against it. Her lips slightly parted, practically begging me to storm across the room and kiss them.

And I almost did just that.

Forcing myself to walk away rather than take her again was harder than what I'm doing to this asshole. That was nearly impossible. This...this is fucking easy in comparison. If I can get my head back in the game.

Focus on the mission. Forget the girl.

I tighten my grip on the knife in my hand and stab into his gut again.

A strangled cry of pain and distress floats out his open mouth and through the warehouse rafters, but there isn't anyone here to hear him or answer his pleas for help. That's why I chose this place. The perfect location to get what I need without drawing unwanted attention.

I squat in front of him, determined to push Vik from my head, reach out with my free hand, and tug on his hair, forcing his head up until his half-closed eyes meet mine. "Let's try this again, shall we?"

He releases a strangled groan, and blood trickles from his lips, down to his bare, cut and bruised chest. "I-I told you...I don't know what you're talking about."

"And I told you that I know you're lying."

This fucker came out of B66 with Kosofik, laughing and joking like old pals. There's no way he doesn't know what's happening with the auction. I don't believe that for one fucking second.

I release his head, and it immediately drops forward, his body too weak to even hold it up. If I'm not careful, I could push this too far to ever get the answers I need. "I'm going to ask you one more time before I switch to another type of persuasion. And if you don't like this"—I flash the knife under the bright overhead fluorescent lights—"you sure as hell aren't gonna like that."

A gurgling objection slips from his lips, and he shakes his head and manages to lift it enough to meet my gaze. "No. No more."

"Then tell me what I need to know."

"Okay..." A rattling, painful-sounding cough makes him double over as much as the bindings allow. If he weren't tied to the chair, he would probably be face down on the ground right now. "I don't know everything. Just that it's happening before the end of the month."

The end of the month?

That doesn't give us much time. Two weeks tops. But it does explain why I haven't gotten a text from Kosofik with the information yet. They likely haven't even decided on a location to hold it or are waiting until the last minute to send instructions to avoid any leaks to the police.

I grin at the man and raise my knife to press my finger against the tip directly in his sightline. "I don't believe you don't know where they're keeping the girls."

Knowing when the auction is going to happen is important, but it doesn't get me to the innocent victims. I need a location, and this guy is going to give it to me.

"You want to know why I know that?" I raise an eyebrow at him. "Because you're buddies with Kosofik, and he runs the show for Yankovich so the big man can keep his hands clean. My guess is, you're his go-to guy, and that means you know every little detail."

Pushing to my feet, I click my tongue and shake my head. "I gave you one opportunity. You're still holding things back from me. Not a wise decision on your part."

One that is going to make this much more painful for him. It's not that I relish this, inflicting pain on others. But when it's a total scumbag like this, I certainly don't feel guilt over it, either.

I grab the bucket of water from the side of my captive's chair and tilt him back to drop his bare feet into it before I snag the jumper cables attached to the car battery sitting on the floor. He sees them and screams, the sound echoing through the vast space but falling to the cold concrete below us without anyone hearing it.

"You can scream all you want." I attach one of the heavy metal clips to his left nipple. That alone is painful enough that he screams again. "Let's see if this changes your cooperation."

I attach the other one to his right nipple, allowing the current to surge through him, his body jerking and twisting painfully as the electricity fries him like an egg from the inside out. His bladder releases in a rush of piss that mixes with the blood on the concrete around the chair.

This type of torture is never pretty, but sometimes, it's necessary to spill some bodily fluids to get some answers. Still, I need him alive enough to give me what I need. I pull one of the cords from him, cut the power, and he sags forward again.

Squatting, I drag his head up by his hair. "Let's try this again. Where are they holding the girls?"

Saliva and blood drip from his lips, and he opens and closes his mouth several times before he finally manages to speak. "I-I-I don't know."

"Really?" This douche canoe is stronger than I gave him credit for. Most men would have broken with the stabbing. Those few who still hung on would have caved to the electrocution. But this fucker still wants to play the game.

I drop his head and reach to reattach the cable to him again, ensuring my motion is still in his line of sight.

His eyes widen, and he sobs and spits. "All I know is it's a warehouse near the docks in Jersey."

A slow smile pulls at my lips. It might not be an address, but it's enough to get me where we need to be. Simply staking out the area around the docks should give us a specific location. The girls need to be fed and kept relatively healthy if they want top dollar for them, so Yankovich's men will need to come and go. That kind of activity can't be hidden easily from someone looking for it specifically.

I reach out and slap the side of his face. "There's a good boy. Was that so hard?

He opens his mouth to answer or say something else, but I reattach the clamp, allowing the current to flow through him again, and wipe the knife off on his jeans before sticking it back into my boot.

"It's been nice knowing ya."

I got what I came here for, and now, it's time to leave. Only what I face when I get back to the loft may be fucking worse than what I did to this guy.

VIKTORIA

I kick against the door near the knob for the thousandth time and release another angry scream when all I get for my efforts is pain shooting up my leg and a twinge in my side. Pressing my hand against the healing wound, I pace away from the door and peek down at the tiny crack between it and the concrete floor.

What lies beyond that door is a mystery, but it seems whoever built this room, they designed it to keep someone in. The solid, sturdy door hasn't budged despite my best efforts to find a weak spot. It's as unwavering as my anger toward Reaper. And not just because he locked me in here but because he did *it* again...managed to sneak in and leave more food for me while I was passed out.

It's almost like he has some sixth sense when to come in here so I won't have the chance to confront him. And even though I've been banging and screaming for what feels like hours, I haven't heard a peep from out there or seen any sort of shadows move in front of the door, which means he probably left me here while he went out to do something no doubt nefarious.

I let out another frustrated growl, wander back to the bed, and plop down on my back.

Bad move.

The entire bed smells like sex. Smells like *him* and what we did...

All the things I don't want to be thinking about right now—not if I want to stay angry.

I need to stay angry.

It's far better than the alternative. Far less dangerous to my heart and sanity.

A low rumble shakes the bed beneath me, and I jerk upright and tilt my head to listen.

The garage door...

It must be right below this room. Wherever he went, he's back. Which means it's time to get myself together.

I jump from the bed and race to the wall by the door, pressing my back flat against it. If he decides to come in here to check on me, I'm going to take advantage of it the only way I can think of.

It may not work. It may not do anything other than piss off Reaper even more, but I still have to try. I can't let him remain in control of the situation, in control of *me*. I have to start thinking of him as what he is—my abductor and a killer—instead of as the man who makes my heart race and my body heat.

Muffled grinding and groaning of the ancient elevator make it through the crack under the door, and then his heavy boots thud on the floor outside the door. A shadow blocks out the light coming under it, and I prepare myself for a fight.

You can do this, Vik. Stay strong.

The lock clicks, and the doorknob turns slowly before the door itself pushes in. I lash out with the only weapon I have in here—my fist. With my police training, I know how to throw a punch. And if it were anyone else, I might have stood a chance, but Reaper's large hand snaps out and wraps around my wrist, stopping it in midair, nowhere near connecting.

He whirls on me and pushes me against the wall so fast that it forces all the air from my lungs in one giant whoosh.

"What the fuck do you think you're doing?" His words come out more growled than spoken. "Did you think that was going to work? Did you actually think you would be able to hurt me enough to get out of here?" A sneer twists his lips. "You clearly don't know who the fuck I am."

I lock my gaze to his, refusing to give even an inch to him as he continues to keep a death-grip on my wrist and pin my other arm between our bodies. "I know exactly who and what you are. You just proved it earlier."

He snarls and leans in until our mouths are only inches from each other. Anger flashes in his blue eyes, making what could be calm pools to swim in tumultuous and stormy. "Then you should know this was a bad move."

"Thinking I won't keep fighting because you fucked me is a bad move on your part."

His brow furrows, his eyes darkening even more. "Is that what you think? That I fucked you to try to stop you from fighting me?"

The incredulous tone in his question tightens my throat, but I force out a response anyway. "It's certainly the way it seems."

He shifts in even closer until we're sharing the same space and breath. "I *fucked* you because I can't get you out of my head. I *fucked* you because even *after* fucking you, I can't get you out of my head. When I needed to focus. When I needed to do my damn job, all I could think about was how fucking beautiful you looked with my cock buried inside you."

My breath catches in my throat, any words I had intended to hurl at him with fury suddenly refusing to leave my lips.

It isn't romantic. It isn't a declaration of love or even that he gives one iota of shit about me or that he keeps me locked up in here like *I'm* the damn criminal. It's a statement about lust—pure animal need. But it's enough to ignite another fire in me that mingles with the anger already burning through my veins and threatening to sear my soul.

Something about this man breaks through the hard exterior I was forced to create to start a new life in a very difficult profession for a woman. I've fought for so long to hide my desires, my needs. To push them down and only give into them in secret when I reached my breaking point. But around Reaper, they flare to life and quickly rage out of control.

I promised myself I wouldn't do this, that I wouldn't let him get close enough to touch me, that I would push him away if it came to this again, but when his lips descend on mine, I don't question it.

Even if I wanted to, I can't...

Instead, I moan into his mouth and issue a low needy-sounding whimper that would make me cringe under any other circumstances.

His hard cock brushes against my hand pinned between us, and I shift my arm the best I can to rub it. He releases my wrist so he can jerk down my pants while I undo his and free him.

He lifts me easily, and I wrap my legs around his waist so he can drive up into me, slamming me back against the wall and shattering any hope I ever had of getting out of this with my heart intact.

13

VIKTORIA

Everything that happened in the last ten minutes blurs into a blissful cloud. But coming down from the orgasmic high, reality slams into me hard and cold despite Reaper's warm body still pressing mine against the wall.

Dammit.

I want to be furious at him. For what just happened. For *everything* that has happened since he entered my life. But that wouldn't be fair. I'm just as much to blame for the situation I find myself in—with his still-hard cock buried inside me, my chest heaving, and my heart aching.

This shouldn't have happened...again, and I could have stopped it at any time. But I didn't even try because as much as I hate him, I also *needed* this. I needed *him* to give me this release from the stress and turmoil and pain of the last few days, even though he's been a major cause of all of it. I need him to remind me that I'm *alive.*

Something about the tension that always builds between

us makes it feel like we're two caustic chemicals that combust when we're thrown together. It's violent and harsh and painful but also brilliant and addictive, like watching a train barreling down the track toward a car stuck there and knowing there isn't any way to stop it yet not being able to look away.

I can't look away from Reaper. I can't give up the way he makes me feel with his body against mine, inside me and enveloping me. But the thought that he might have been gone the last few hours, doing something I should be arresting him for, yet I just did *that* with him, won't let me hold in the question that keeps floating through my head.

Over and over and over again...

And I can't just let it go.

I swallow against my dry throat and turn my head until my lips brush against his ear, where his head is still buried against my neck. "Where were you?"

His entire body goes rigid, and he slowly pulls back his head until his hard eyes meet mine. He raises his hand from my side and captures my face in his rough palm, brushing his thumb across my cheek. "My dick is still inside you and you're asking where I was?"

Shit.

The last thing I expected was to hear hurt lacing his words. Anger—yes. Reaper seems to harbor a lot of that. But the fact that my question might actually put a ding in the armor he wears so diligently never even crossed my mind. Not after he walked away and locked me back up in this room earlier today.

Such an easy dismissal of what happened between us left me unnerved and bitter. Still, I never imagined it had affected him in *any* way. He certainly never showed it before now, only acted like it didn't mean anything to him other than a way to get a needed release. I never intended to hurt him, even though he hurt *me* by disappearing.

Why couldn't I keep my mouth shut for one damn minute? Enjoy a few moments of peace and revel in the afterglow of really hot sex?

I glance down, avoiding his penetrating gaze, and my focus goes right to his boots...and the dark stains splattered on them. It's a stark reminder of why I asked the question in the first place. Because I know enough about Reaper to know he wasn't out on a walk, enjoying the scenery and people of the Garden State while I was locked up in here.

My resolve returning, I lift my head and meet his stare. "Yes, I want to know where you were and how you got blood all over your boots."

A low growl rumbles in his chest and vibrates through mine straight to my heart. Heat blazes in his blue eyes, far different from what was there before. This heat is born of fury.

At me asking or because of what he did?

He shifts slightly, his cock still buried inside me, and I squeeze around him instinctively and issue a low groan.

His hand tightens on my face, drawing me closer to him. "I just spent a few hours of quality time with one of Yankovich's men to get the information we need, and even while I was there, doing things that would make you cringe, even *then,* I couldn't get you out of my fucking head."

I couldn't get you out of my fucking head...

He's trying to distract me. Get me to focus on *those* words and what they might mean instead of the other part of that explanation, the part that goes to my very important question.

"Yankovich's man? What did you find out?"

Reaper watches me for a moment, searching my face for

something he apparently doesn't find because he releases a heavy sigh and moves his hand from my cheek to the wall behind me. "The auction is happening at the end of the month. And I have a pretty good idea where the girls are now."

My breath catches in my throat. It's exactly what we've been looking for, what we need to finalize our plans and make a move. We can finally free these innocent women, but Reaper's comment from earlier still lingers at the forefront of my brain with the visual of the splatter on his boots.

A few hours of quality time...

I glance at his hand against the wall, and while there isn't any blood on it, that doesn't mean anything with this man. He knows how to clean up after himself, how to do a dirty deed and not leave anything that will tie him to it. I'm sure his clothes and boots will end up in some incinerator in the bowels of this building as soon as he pulls his dick from inside me.

"Did you..." I swallow and force myself to hold his gaze, even though doing so makes my heart thunder against my ribcage violently. "Kill him?"

His anger returns, flaring to life, darkening his eyes and tensing his shoulders. "So what if I did? He was a piece of shit who got what he deserved. That's all you need to know. Everything *I* needed to know before I took care of business."

Took care of business.

"Are you admitting to a cop that you just murdered someone?"

A cold grin tilts his lips. "I'm not admitting anything. You can draw your own conclusions, but what are you going to do?" One of his dark eyebrows rises. "Turn me in?"

Would I? Could I really turn him in for killing some piece-of-

shit lackey of Yankovich who is involved in a human trafficking ring and likely even worse?

For a brief moment, I consider saying no, but then the entire reason I became a cop in the first place slams into my brain, altering my response, which comes out with more bite than I intend, unable to restrain my incredulity.

"Yes, Reaper, I would." Tightening my grip on his shirt, I tug on the fabric to emphasize my point. "Who made *you* judge, jury, and executioner? What gives *you* the right to decide who is guilty of what, what their penance should be, and then complete their ultimate sentence?"

Reaper leans in slowly, and the absolute calm that overcomes his face sends a chill through my spine, making me shiver. The movement only shifts his cock still buried in me even deeper, and I bite back a whimper rather than admit how good it feels while we're having this argument.

His lips brush against mine, just barely, enough to leave me wanting more but not giving it to me. "*I* did, Vik. And I'm more than qualified. I've spent my entire adult life hunting down threats to this country and threats to innocent people all over the fucking world. I know evil when I see it. I can *smell* it coming from them while I watch them in hiding. I can *feel* it in my gut when I look into their eyes. These men deserve to pay the ultimate price for what they've done. And if the big man upstairs has any issue with what I'm doing in my life, He can tell me Himself when I finally head to the pearly gates...or, if I find myself in the nine circles of Hell, I'll have my answer."

He brings his hand back to my face and squeezes my jaw.

"Until then, Vik, I'm just going to keep doing what I can to make this world a safer place. If you want to stop me, you can certainly try, but you won't get very far or be very successful. I think I just proved that."

To emphasize his point, he drives into me hard, pushing his cock as deep inside as humanly possible and completely stealing my breath or any response I have.

Instead, a small gasp tumbles from my lips, and I fight the urge to beg him to go. To move. To fuck me hard again.

Don't give in, Vik. Don't let him take this control.

I force myself to open my eyes and hold his searing gaze. "Turning you in or stopping you would require me getting out of here, and you don't seem inclined to let that happen anytime soon."

His lips twitch as he fights a smile. "No, I am not so inclined."

"But you know where the girls are. Let me help you plan a way to get them back safely."

He shakes his head, leaning in again until his warm breath flutters against my lips. "I have all the help I need. What I need you to do is stay here and stay safe."

"Hank will be looking for me."

"I've dealt with Hank."

"What?"

"I took care of him."

Any hope I had for rescue deflates with that revelation. "So no one is coming for me..."

"It certainly appears that way."

"And you're just going to keep me locked up here."

He tightens his hold on my jaw. "I'm going to do whatever I have to with you to make sure you keep your ass alive and out of trouble."

"Don't you think it's a little late for that?"

I don't know if I'm referring to what already happened with Yankovich and his men or what just happened a few hours ago between Reaper and me, what is *currently* happening between us.

It seems his answer is the same either way. "Damn right it is."

REAPER

I growl the words at Vik like a rabid dog about to bite, barely restraining my desire to lash out at her even more, but I don't care how menacing I may look or sound right now. It's necessary. Her pussy clenches around my cock, practically begging for more, and the woman *still* can't stop arguing with me.

She just isn't getting it.

Viktoria just can't seem to understand how bad this is for both of us, but especially for her.

"You've been nothing *but* trouble since the moment I met you, Vik. First, letting your partner drag you to B66 without the department knowing or having any backup, a place you knew there was a possibility you might be recognized. Then, you two tried to grab me, thinking you would get something from me and wasted time you could have used investigating the real criminals. *Then*, you had to follow Hank and get yourself *shot*. *Then*, you didn't stay at the club where Celeste and the Knights could take care of you, and instead, you went home where you would've bled out had I not been there. A home that is so easy to break in to that it was a fucking *joke* to think you'd be safe there. And then you did the stupidest thing you could have. You let me *kiss* you."

My dick twitches inside her at the memory of the first

time I got a taste of her, that first press of my lips to hers. I capture her face between both my palms and tilt her face up to ensure she's one hundred percent with me on how *stupid* she's been.

"And let's not forget that you *then* got yourself kidnapped."

Her eyes widen slightly. "By *you!*"

"Again, you're fucking welcome for that. But even kidnapped, even knowing your life is in danger and *why* I took you, you just can't seem to stay away from trouble."

Instead, she runs headlong into it and deals with the ramifications only after the fact. But it's time I force her to really think about what she's doing, what we're doing, and what it means for her future.

Her mouth falls open, and a gasp slips from those lips I want to kiss so badly. "*You're* the one who kissed *me.*"

True...

But I'm not about to take all the responsibility for this. "You could've said *no*. You *should* have said no...because I'm trouble, Viktoria. You already know that. You've known it since the moment you saw me in that bar. And yet, look where we are...again."

I drag back my hips and plunge into her again just to prove my point. Even though we just fucked five minutes ago and I haven't pulled my dick from her warm cunt, I still haven't had enough of her. I don't know that it's even possible to.

She groans, dropping her head back, and tightens her hands in my shirt, clinging to me.

"We just *fucked,* Vik, and I'm still *inside* you and we're arguing about what I just did to one of Yankovich's men and whether or not you're going to turn me into the damn police." I shake my head. "This isn't healthy or normal at all,

Viktoria. *I* am not healthy or normal. I'm fucked up and volatile, and I would *destroy* you."

It's the only warning I can give her. The only way I can try to make her understand what she's doing to herself by being with me like this. If I told her what it's doing to me, how it makes me weak to have a blind spot where she's concerned when I need to stay focused on my mission, it would only confuse things more. This needs to be about *her,* about how wrong this is for *her* and how it will decimate her future.

Her glassy eyes meet mine. "Maybe I want to be destroyed."

"Fuck." I fight the desire to fuck her silent, stopping my hips from pulling back and driving into her relentlessly until she can't breathe, let alone speak. "Don't say shit like that to me, Viktoria. You think you know what I can do, but you can't even fathom what I have done in my past. You need to stay as far away from me as you can."

Run away...

I swallow through the strange emotion clogging my throat. "I'm dangerous. To you. To your career. Because I'm not going to stop. I'm not going to stop taking out these assholes who deserve it. I'm not going to stop doing what I can to protect people who need it. I'm not going to put you in a position to have to choose between your morals and *me.* I could never forgive myself if you chose me over everything you've worked your entire life for." I shake my head and squeeze my eyes closed. "I'm not worth any of that, Vik. Not even fucking close."

A silence lingers between us, heavy with the weight of all that I've just confessed to her. Then her soft, warm hand releases my shirt and presses to my cheek, and she forces my face up. I open my eyes to find hers shimmering with unshed tears, and I start to pull away from her, from the wall, to put some distance between us. But she reaches up and clings to the back of my neck with both hands, wrapping her legs more tightly around me, keeping me buried inside her.

"Shouldn't I be the one who decides what you're worth? Isn't it *my* life and therefore my decision?"

She rolls her hips and squeezes my dick tightly in her wet heat. I grit my teeth against the very real desire to drive into her hard again, to somehow show her how dangerous I can really be. How badly I can hurt her.

Her soft lips brush against my cheek. "Does what I want not matter? How I feel not matter?"

"Fuck. Of course, it does. I'm trying to keep you from throwing away your entire life. Why can't you see that?"

She pulls one hand down from around my neck and presses it over my heart. "What I see is a man who has been scarred by what he's had to do in his life. A man who has such a tainted view of the world and the people in it that he can't even see the good anymore. But I also see a man who would never hurt me."

My chest tightens, my breaths suddenly harder to drag in. I shake my head. "Don't be so sure about that, Viktoria."

"I *am* sure. And maybe there isn't a future for us. Maybe when this is all over, you'll disappear and I'll go back to being a cop with a heavy weight on my conscience. But that's *my* decision to make, not yours." She drops her forehead against mine. "I get to make the choice of what's good for me or what isn't. And in this moment, I choose you. It might be different tomorrow, might be different the day after that, but it's my choice and mine alone. So, please, Reaper...fuck me."

"Christ, Viktoria." I pull my head back and lift her chin,

swiping away a single stray tear from her cheek with my thumb. "You don't know what you're asking me for."

"Yes." She nods slowly, her bottom lip trembling. "Yes, I do."

She's asking me to break her. To demolish everything she stands for in this world to have a few minutes of comfort and bliss in each other's arms. She's asking me to do this, knowing we can't have a future, knowing that when this is over, I'll walk away and never look back.

Even with all that assured, she still leans forward and presses her lips to mine slowly, tentatively, almost like she's expecting me to pull away and run.

But I don't have the strength for that left. Not by a fucking long shot.

14

REAPER

The consistent soft rise and fall of Viktoria's chest assures me she's asleep, but I still wait a few minutes, watching her, just to be safe, before I gently pull my arm out from under her and climb from the bed to hastily tug on my jeans and slip from the room.

I close the door quietly but don't bother locking it this time. I'm not going anywhere today. Too hard to do what I need to do in daylight. Plus, I don't think Viktoria would make the mistake of trying to escape again.

Not after what happened the last time she tried something so stupid.

Scrubbing my hands over my face, I try to rub away the visuals of how she looked at me while I had her pinned against the wall, and splayed out on the bed, and bent over the end of it. It doesn't work. They're burned into my retinas and mind forever. I force my eyes open and stare at the chipped paint on the door.

What the hell are we doing?

I don't even know. Part of me screams to go back in there, climb into bed with her again, and take her as many times as possible before I have to make the next move in my mission. But the bigger part of me is telling me to lock the door and keep it locked this time. Because if she's in there and I'm out here, *that* can't happen again. And the more it *does* happen, the harder it's going to be to walk away when this is all over. The harder it's going to be not to worry about what it might do to her career when we finally have to pull the trigger on these guys.

But I can't worry about that right now. I need to get in touch with Hank and let him know what I got from Yankovich's guy and try to find out when Chaos and Mouth will get here.

First, I need a fucking smoke.

I cross the loft to the far side, unlock and push up the old window, and step through it out to my usual spot, where I've found myself more times than I can count since I first met Vik and her nosy partner. The fire escape is the only spot in this entire place where I can't smell her, where every breath isn't full of that soft, flowery scent that makes me taste her on my tongue.

Even the heaviest drag from my cigarette and holding the smoke in my lungs can't erase that.

Why do I even try?

Instead of contemplating that question, I pull out my phone and call Grayson. The sooner I get him updated on what I learned, the quicker I can focus on finding the exact location and creating a plan of attack that might bring those women home to their families alive.

The determined detective answers on the third ring. "Dixon? Is Vik all right?"

Her screams from earlier fill my ears again, and I clench

my jaw but manage to grit out a response through my teeth. "Fine. I got something. I know where the girls might be."

"Talk to me. Where?"

"A warehouse in Newark, looks like somewhere near the Jersey docks. I don't have an address, but that narrows down our search by a fucking lot."

"Makes sense. Still a pretty large scope, though. The waterfront is adjacent to the airport. You got the Port Newark Container Terminal and the Redhook Container Terminal there, too. Easy access to move the girls after the auction. You want me to have the Satan's Knights recon the area?"

"No. I have a few buddies coming in to help. Let us do it. No offense to your friends on the motorcycles, but they're not the most inconspicuous group."

Hank grunts as I take another drag off my cigarette and blow smoke out into the air.

"It shouldn't be hard for us to find the right warehouse fairly quickly. The auction is happening at the end of the month, so we have time to determine the exact location, get any blueprints we can of the building, and plan before we go in there."

"How sure are you about the auction being at the end of the month?"

"Why?"

"Well, I got Anastasia to cooperate. I can't take all the credit, though. I think Parrish put the fear of God in her. The woman doesn't want her kids to have to relive the shit they witnessed when Parrish and the Knights took out their father, so in exchange for their protection, she's been talking. Told me Michail mentioned a charity gala to her, but she doesn't buy it. And after doing some research of my own, neither do I. "

A charity gala?

Seems a bit odd for someone like Yankovich, but it sounds like Hank knows even more. "Explain."

"Well, when he first mentioned this gala to her, she got suspicious because he's never committed to one specific charity. Any donation made is for tax purposes. Now, all of a sudden, he's hosting one? I checked out his financials, and she's right. I also looked into each specific charity he's donated to, and not a single one has a gala on their calendar. I've been to a couple of these fundraisers for the Sergeants Benevolent Association, and I can tell you, not only do they advertise the fuck out of them, they charge per plate. She also said Michail beefed up his security. He took the two guards he had detailing her and the kids and put them on him."

"So you think the gala is a front for the auction?"

"It could be. It could also be a fucking decoy. Ana overheard him and Kosofik talking about me and the Knights. That's how she knew who I was when I approached her. If he thinks we're onto him, he could be staging this gala to coincide with the auction. He sends Kosofik to the warehouse in Newark while he wines and dines the elite at B66. That gives him an alibi and me no arrest. The sale takes place, and he gets off."

"Fuck."

"Yeah, that's why I'm asking you if you're sure this auction is set for the end of the month because Anastasia called me last night from the burner phone I gave her and said the gala is in four days."

"If your theory is correct, then we need to be ready to strike."

"We need that location."

"I'll get it."

"Are you—"

"I said I'll get it."

"Fine." Hank pauses for a beat. "You share any of this with Vik?"

"She knows what she needs to know."

"Oh, yeah, how's that going for you?"

I pinch the bridge of my nose and shake my head. "She wants to be there, but I told her there wasn't any fucking way I was letting her near this raid."

He laughs. "I bet that went over well."

"Of course not. But I'm not about to let her tank her career to help us with this. You were already in bed with the Satan's Knights. Whether that move was right or wrong, you made the choice yourself. Vik was kind of dragged into this kicking and screaming. You know this doesn't sit right with her, even if the reason behind it is valid."

He sighs, the sound just as heavy with frustration as what I'm feeling. "Yeah, I know. If you can keep her away from this, then do it. You're right. When all this comes to a head, I'm going to have a big mess with the department on my hands, and I'd rather take that heat than have her do it."

At least we're on the same page.

Protecting Vik is just as important at this point as finding the women being held by the Russians.

And I fucking hate myself for it.

How could I let a woman get into my head like this?

It's a weakness I could never afford and one I managed to avoid for a decade. Yet do one favor for an old friend and I somehow find myself drowning in unwanted feelings that only complicate the job I came here to do. A job made all that much harder when I'm doing it alone while keeping my eye on the loaded pistol locked in that bedroom.

"My buddies should arrive in the next day or two, and I'll

start without them. We'll get the precise location ASAP, and I'll keep you updated."

"Sounds good. If I get any more intel on the gala, I'll reach out."

I end the call and immediately send a text to Mouth.

ETA?

Tomorrow sometime. Chaos?

Calling him now to confirm but should be around the same.

It can't come soon enough.

Maybe with the boys around, it will provide the distraction I need to keep my hands off and my dick out of Viktoria.

I dial Chaos and wait for him to pick up, taking several long drags off my cigarette before he finally answers.

"Yep."

"ETA?"

"Just wrapping up a few things. Tomorrow, day after at the latest."

"Good. I need the backup."

He chuckles. "For the vermin or for the girl?"

"Shit." I shake my head and toss it back to stare up at the clouds passing slowly in the blue sky. "This girl, man...you'll see what I'm talking about when you get here."

He barks out a laugh—wherever he is, he clearly isn't concerned about making noise. "If she's got *you* this twisted up, she must be something."

"Oh, she's something, all right. A big fucking pain in my ass."

"If that were true, you wouldn't be so worried and twisted up."

"There's nothing to worry about as long as I can keep her out of trouble."

"That sounds ominous. Can't wait to hear about what's going on. See you soon, brother."

He ends the call, and I set my phone on the step beside me and finish my cigarette, trying to relax as much as possible and enjoy the last smoke I'll have for a while since I need to start recon.

As soon as it gets dark, I'll head out to the area around the docks and see if I can narrow down and exclude the warehouses until the guys get here.

Which means locking that door I just came out of again.

Something twists in my gut at the thought of doing that to her, but it's the right thing to do. The only way to keep her safe—at least from the things on the outside that could hurt her.

When it comes to me, it seems that door and lock just aren't enough.

VIKTORIA

A big fucking pain in my ass...

Reaper's words echo through my head even though he ended the call a few minutes ago, and anger only continues to tighten my fists at my sides where I'm pressed against the wall beside the open window that leads out to the fire escape.

It's not that I'm surprised to hear he feels that way— after all, he's basically said the same to my face—but whoever he's talking to doesn't know me, doesn't know the situation we're in. And while I only caught the end of the conversation, it's clear their only opinion of me is going to be formed based on the less-than-flattering statements Reaper just made.

As if it isn't bad enough he's planning on keeping me away from the rescue of the girls, now his friends are going to think it's because I'm some idiot who can't watch her own back or protect herself.

The fact that Reaper was so easily able to grab me off the street and keep me locked up here doesn't help my case.

But that was *then*, and this is *now*.

I'm physically and mentally stronger. More determined to help those girls and prove myself to Reaper. Ready to face whatever consequences may come from whatever actions I have to take.

And while I may have been on the fence about that not too long ago—wavering between ratting the guys out to the department before anyone gets hurt or joining them in their mission—I'm one hundred percent convinced now about what I have to do.

It's the only thing I can *do.*

Reaper thinks he's keeping me from danger by locking me up in that damn room, but all he's done is awaken a sleeping giant. He's made me more intent than ever to prove what I'm capable of and use my skills to help those girls.

I force myself to uncurl my fists to avoid making my palms bleed, and the sound of Reaper moving out on the old metal fire escape makes me still.

If I really wanted to, I could probably sneak back into the room and pretend to be sleeping before he even realizes I came out and overheard him, but I don't want to play games with him. The only way I'll ever get anywhere with

Reaper is to face him head-on and prove I'm not going to roll over just because he puts on a show of being scary and macho.

He doesn't scare me. If anything, my heart aches for the man I can see hiding behind the scarred surface. He would rather be called Reaper than go by the name his parents gave him. He would rather be a monster, someone to fear and look over your shoulder for, than be human and everything that comes with that.

Footsteps creak the metal just outside the window, and he climbs in and immediately turns to face me.

"Not going to try to hit me this time?" His gaze darts down to my hands at my sides.

I cross my arms over my chest and square my shoulders. "No. I'm done physically fighting you because that's a battle I won't win. I'm moving on to a war of logic."

One of his dark eyebrows rises slowly. "Logic?"

Nodding, I take a step toward him. "Yes, logic. You may want to keep me locked up in there." I wave a hand absently across the room toward the open door. "But you *need* me with you at that warehouse when you finally raid it. You need as many skilled shooters as possible. And you need a woman who can talk to the girls and make sure they understand they're safe. Do you really think they'll trust a bunch of guys storming in wearing all black or Satan's Knights' cuts after they watch you slaughter whoever is holding them?"

His lips twist slightly, but he doesn't respond, just crosses his arms over his bare chest, emphasizing the hard, lean muscle and scars dotted across his lightly tanned skin.

"You *need* me there, Reaper. Whether you want to admit it or not. And keeping me locked up here won't stop you from worrying or thinking about me or whatever other lame excuse you come up with to justify it."

His blue eyes darken almost to black, his clenched jaw twitching.

Shit.

I hadn't intended to let loose on him like that, and I may have spoken a little too much truth for him to handle right now—or maybe ever. Something tells me Reaper isn't a man who likes to be forced to face anything involving "feelings" or to have his authority questioned.

And I'm certainly doing that right now.

Maybe to my own detriment. Reaper could literally throw me over his shoulder—again—and toss me back in that room and lock it without a look back.

He more than *could,* actually. He probably *will.*

But instead of going all caveman on me, Reaper sucks in a deep breath and blows it out slowly, like he's trying to rein himself back in and contain his desire to lash out at me like he has before.

I raise an eyebrow at him in question, waiting for him to respond.

Finally, he shakes his head. "Even if I agree with your assessment—and that is a *big* if—you're forgetting the fact that you're a cop. You're going to ruin your entire career for *this*?"

What's he talking about? Me and him or my involvement with this entire case?

Either way, my answer remains the same.

I hold his hard gaze, letting the silence linger between us a few moments longer than I normally would, trying to find any hint that might tell me what his question was about. But just like always, Reaper remains stoic, hard, never giving away anything that's going on inside his head. The momentary crack in the wall he's built up around himself that I saw earlier has closed up as if it never existed.

But I know it did. I saw it. Saw the way he snapped and lost control. The way we both did.

"It's worth it."

That's all I can think to say because the more time I spend with Reaper, the longer I contemplate what those girls must be going through, the more confident I become that this is the right course of action.

Of course, seeing the scumbags responsible have to face a courtroom would bring a certain sense of justice, but it wouldn't put an end to what's happening. Not with the size of network Yankovich has. If we don't prove how serious we are about shutting down this trafficking ring, if we don't spill blood, someone else will just pick up in his place.

We need to make a statement. Prove that we're willing to go to any means to make these men pay and protect the innocent.

If that means I lose my badge, so be it. I'll do everything in my power to keep it, but I'm not going to kid myself into believing that anything we do is going to be by the book or even legal.

"I'm ready to face the consequences, Reaper. I'm ready to do whatever it takes." I point back toward the open door of the bedroom. "You've had me in that room for days, and you want to know what I've been thinking about in there?"

He watches me with hooded eyes, his arms still crossed over his chest that somehow seems bigger now than ever. The corner of his mouth twitches, giving me a clear indication of what he *thinks* I've been thinking about.

I push my finger right in between his hard pecs. "Besides how *mad* I am at you, I've been thinking about what it must be like for those women locked away somewhere, knowing what fate awaits them and what terror it will be. At least here, I know you won't hurt me and that I'll get released after a while. But they know the opposite is true for them. And as distraught as I've been, it pales in comparison to what they must be feeling."

My stomach clenches even considering the pain and terror they're living in, and I press my palm flat against his warm skin.

Reaper freezes under my touch but does nothing to push me away, even as my fingers brush over a scar.

"Let me help you free those women. I have to do this."

His lips twisting, Reaper watches me for a moment, searching my eyes for fear or regret, for anything else that might tell him I'm second-guessing this decision, but he won't find it there because there is no second-guessing it. This is what *has* to happen.

"Don't fight me on this, Roderick. You know I can help."

Using his real name might be playing dirty, especially combined with my hand over his heart and stepping even closer into his space. But finally, after what feels like an eternity, he uncrosses his arms from in front of him and reaches up to cup my cheek.

"If I let you do this, if I let you come with us, I need you by my side the entire time. Where I can see you. Where I can *know* you're okay. I'm not going to take any chances with you. If I tell you to get the fuck out, you get the fuck out."

I open my mouth to argue with him, but he shakes his head and tightens his grip, using it to drag me up against his firm body.

"Don't argue with me, Vik. This isn't something I'll change my mind about. It's the only way this is going to happen, so either you accept my terms, or you go back in that room to keep fighting me only to have nothing change."

"I don't want to fight with you." I bring my other hand up to rest over his steadily beating heart. "Not when I feel like fighting is all I've been doing my entire life. First, against what the neighborhood expected of me. Then, against Mom and Dad and Anya when I left to find a better life. Then, against the men at the precinct who didn't think I could handle my job. Now you. I just want to stop fighting."

"No." He shakes his head again and leans in, brushing his lips against mine. "Don't stop fighting. Just change who you're fighting against. We have a common enemy, Vik. So, let's take them out together."

15

REAPER

I t's strange to come back and see the bedroom open. Having it closed since I brought Vik here has given me a much-needed barrier against all the turmoil that woman brings to my mission and my body. The non-stop bombardment of sass and sexiness from her drives me to want to simultaneously pin her against the wall and fuck her silent again or lock that door permanently. But I left it open when I took off to recon the warehouses in the area around the docks. Vik isn't going anywhere. Not after I agreed to allow her to help with the mission.

Hearing her words, seeing how much being involved and helping those girls means to her, I couldn't deny her that, even if it means having to keep an eye on her while decimating the Russians. But that doesn't mean I was about to let her come with me while I was trying to zero in on our target. Not when she still has one on her back.

The fact that she didn't fight me when I told her she was staying almost felt like some sort of trick, like she was playing a game with me. Yet, for some reason, I trust her. She won't interfere with our plans. Whatever reservations she had about our mission have been erased by the time she spent in that room.

It wasn't my plan, but it is a nice side effect.

Because she's right. Having another trained shooter along will be invaluable. As long as she stays on my six and doesn't run off to play hero and end up getting herself hurt again.

I couldn't live with that—seeing her in pain and bleeding again. Even thinking about it makes my ribcage feel like it's tightening around my lungs, making it impossible to breathe.

Whatever is going on between us, it's affecting me more than I want to acknowledge, deeper than I ever want to explore.

Just knowing she would be here, waiting when I got back, sent a strange warmth through my entire body while I was sneaking from building to building, checking for any signs of Yankovich's crew.

Is this what it felt like for the guys who had women to come home to?

All those years, all I ever thought about was how much it would hurt someone who loved me to have me gone. To be constantly worrying and wondering if I was all right. To not know for days or even weeks at a time that I was alive and breathing. The devastation it would cause if I didn't come home.

Keeping those worries at the forefront of my brain made it easier to walk away from all the women I slept with. It made it possible to prevent myself from letting anyone get close. But it never crossed my mind that the good might outweigh the bad. That having someone care about you that deeply could offer you something you can't find anywhere else—a reason to live. And somehow, that woman, the one tearing my world apart from the inside out, has made me question everything.

It doesn't keep me away, though. I'm drawn toward the sound of the running water in the small bathroom attached to the "prison" that's become hers. I kick off my boots and cross the floor into the room, listening for any signs she's been alerted to my return. But all I hear is the rush of the shower and a low, melodic hum from deep in her throat that goes straight to my cock.

I hope Vik got some sleep after I left because things are going to get a lot busier and a lot more complicated very soon. Our time together will end as soon as Yankovich is taken care of, and I'm not about to waste one minute of it. These moments need to last me a lifetime.

All I can think about while I undress is getting under that cascade of water with her, how beautiful she'll look with it trickling over her breasts and down between her thighs. Taking my hard cock in hand, I step into the small steamy room. The frosted glass door offers me the perfect view of all of Vik's luscious curves as she turns her back to the water and tilts her head under it.

Fuck...

My cock aches to be inside her again, and I stroke it slowly, watching her rinse her hair while she hums to herself contently.

"Are you just going to stand there jerking off, or are you going to join me?"

Her question freezes my hand, and I can't fight off the grin that pulls at my lips.

Such a smartass.

It's okay, though. I'll just fuck it out of her.

And enjoy every fucking second of it.

I slide open the shower door and meet her bright-green eyes, dancing with amusement. She knows what she just said is likely to set me off, and she doesn't care. Vik likes poking the bear.

She raises an eyebrow at me, the water pelting her back and steam rising around her. "How did it go?"

Stepping in, I shake my head. "Good. But I don't want to talk about that right now."

I close the distance between us and wrap my arms around her slick body, letting my hands drift down to grab her ass.

She brings her arms up around my neck and drags my head down to press her mouth to mine. "Oh, yeah, what do you want to do?"

Her tongue probes playfully at my lips, and I grind my cock against her stomach and enjoy her little mewl of need filling the tight space. I drop my hand between her legs and feel the slick heat of her pussy, so wet and ready for me.

Driving inside her right now sounds incredible, but there's something else I need to do first. She wraps her hand around my cock, and I drag my mouth back from hers and shake my head.

"Not yet, Vik."

Before she can protest too much, I drop to my knees onto the cracked tile of the shower and slide my tongue where my fingers just were.

Good God.

Her arousal coats my tongue and makes me almost come on the spot. Even after fucking Vik a half a dozen times over the last couple of days, I'm still dancing along that razor-thin edge of losing control like a fumbling teenager the first time he touches a woman's cunt.

But I won't embarrass myself by reaching the end before she does. Determined to make her come hard and fast, I lap at her relentlessly, savoring her taste and committing it to memory.

She gasps and grabs my shoulders to hold herself steady, but I plan on devouring this woman so well she won't be able to stand, so I push her backward until her shoulders and ass press against the wall. With the hot spray beating against my back, I dip my head down to taste her again. She moans and digs her nails in my shoulders, the sharp bite of pain making me groan against her wet flesh and drive my tongue into her while I slip my thumb up across her clit.

Her hips buck against my face, pushing herself tighter against me, seeking the very thing I'm just as desperate to give her.

I could eat this woman forever and never have my fill. I don't care if I suffocate like this. At least I would die a happy man.

Yet, it still isn't enough. I grasp her thighs and lift her to settle them over my shoulders, spreading her pussy wide open right in front of my face, exactly where I want it. But she needs more. I pull my tongue from inside her and replace it with my fingers, curling them to find that perfect spot inside while I swirl my tongue on her clit and allowing her the ability to roll her hips and drive up against my mouth and hand.

She offers a little mewl of approval as I suck her clit between my lips and flick my tongue against it. One of her hands moves from my shoulder to dig into my hair, grasping at the short locks, searching for something to cling to.

I chuckle against her pussy, the vibration sending her wild, her hips seeking the release she's so close to—that I'm so close to. My cock aches so badly, it can't be ignored anymore. I reach down with my free hand and grasp it, stroking it hard and fast as I eat her like she's my last meal. Because this very well might be the last time we get to do this.

Once Chaos and Mouth get here, things will move quickly, and I'm not ready to stop until she comes all over my face and screams my name loud enough that the echo will remain with me forever.

VIKTORIA

Whatever has suddenly gotten into Reaper, it's both terrifying and exhilarating at the same time. He once told me he will always complete his mission, and it seems his mission now is to drive me to the brink of insanity without giving me release.

He lashes at my clit with his tongue while he pumps his fingers into me, but it isn't enough. Not nearly enough. I need him inside me. I need that feeling of completeness, of being whole and filled that only his dick can give me. But Reaper doesn't seem inclined to offer me that. Just torture me.

And damn, is he good at his job.

Squeezing my thighs around his head, I drag him closer, desperate for more friction, more force, more everything, and when he sucks my clit between his lips in that pulsating rhythm, my body detonates like an atom bomb going off. My pussy clenches around his fingers, clasping and seeking what it really wants. His moan of approval against my skin only makes my orgasm surge on longer, and Reaper refuses to offer me any reprieve from the relentlessness of his mouth.

I claw at the back of his head, simultaneously wanting to draw him closer and push him away because of the intensity of the feelings flooding my system. Every muscle vibrates, spasming with pleasure and need and something else I've never felt before.

When the orgasm finally subsides and I sag back against the cold tiles, Reaper looks up at me with a hooded gaze filled with promise, his lips glistening with my release. He darts out his tongue across them, his shoulder bunching and flexing under my thigh as he strokes his cock.

His blue eyes locked with mine, his jaw tightens, and he comes on a low groan, hot spurts hitting my ass where it's dipped down low against the tile.

Fuck. Why is that so hot?

Reaper got so turned on by going down on me that he just came without even getting inside me. But the look he's giving me now suggests we're far from through. He slowly slides my legs from his shoulders, lowers my feet to the tile, and holds me steady with a solid grip on my hips as he rises to his feet, his breathing heavy.

"Christ, Vik..."

I don't even know how to respond, but I don't have to because he captures my mouth in a searing kiss and grinds his still-hard cock against my stomach.

"Turn around."

It isn't a request. It's an order. And I do it on shaking legs to press my hands against the tile and arch my back, offering myself to him.

He grips my hip firmly with one hand, aligns his cock with the other, and slams up into me, pushing my chest against the wall while the hot water still beats against his back.

I gasp and press my cheek to the cool tile surface, a startling juxtaposition to the heat of his body against mine and filling me. He leans forward and places his hands over mine, twining our fingers as he drills into me, hitting exactly the right spot to make me lose control all over again.

His warm lips kiss a trail up my neck and across my cheek until his hot breath flutters against my ear. "Whatever happens, we'll always have this."

My heart thunders against my rib cage, the rush of the water falling filling my ears while his cock continues to drill into me like there is no tomorrow.

Maybe that's what his words mean.

He knows this might be our last time together. That thought makes tears form in my eyes, but I don't want him to stop, especially not now. Not when my body tingles with the rise of another orgasm. Not when I'm so damn close.

One of his hands pulls free of mine, and Reaper captures my chin and turns my head back to meet his gaze. "Look at me when you come."

The low growl of the words sends a jolt straight to my clit, and almost as if he can read my mind, he releases my chin and reaches down there, working his hand in time with the pace and punishment of his cock.

That's exactly what I need to release another cataclysmic orgasm that leaves me gasping and shaking as he pumps into me harder and deeper and finally comes again deep inside me, never taking his eyes off mine.

I sag back against him, this tiny shower suddenly feeling far too large, like there's too much space between us, and he wraps his arms around me and buries his face against the crook of my neck.

He places a kiss there, and I release a tiny, contented sigh that's interrupted by loud clapping filling the bathroom. We both jerk our heads toward the steamed glass door, two shadowy figures barely visible through it.

"Wow. That was hot. Way to go, man."

Reaper issues a low growl and turns to place his body between me and whoever is standing out there. "Get the fuck out of here, you asshole."

I glance up at him. "Who the hell is that?"

He sighs and squeezes closed his eyes. "That was Chaos."

"Chaos?"

Somehow, that name doesn't seem to bode well for what's to come.

16

REAPER

They're on me the second I step out of the bedroom and close the door behind me, not giving a shit about the fact that I'm standing in front of them buck naked.

Chaos motions behind me. "Whoa, dude, you didn't tell me you were banging her or that she was so hot."

I glare at him as I make my way to the other bedroom to grab some clothes, both of them hot on my trail. "You didn't have to be a total prick about it."

"Sorry, man." He holds up his hands even though he doesn't mean the apology and chuckles. "I can't believe you didn't hear my bike outside when I pulled up, or the garage door, or the elevator coming up."

I pull a pair of jeans from a drawer and jerk them on, then do the same with a T-shirt. "I'm suddenly regretting giving you guys keys to this place."

The safehouse was meant to be somewhere we could all use when needed, not a place for them to come give me shit when I finally manage to get it in with a beautiful woman after six months of self-imposed celibacy.

Chaos chuckles and leans against the door jamb while Mouth watches from just behind him, a smirk curling his lips.

I point at Mouth. "You could have given me some warning."

Like a fucking text saying they were going to arrive soon...

He shrugs and shakes his head as if to say, *"What the hell was I supposed to do?"*

A fucking text would have been nice.

I wave them off and intentionally bump shoulders with Chaos as I make my way out of the bedroom and into the main living space of the loft. They follow me to the kitchen, and each takes a stool at the counter while I grab a bottle of water from the fridge and chug it. "I would offer you two fuckers a beer, but..." I shrug.

Chaos' lips twitch. "Still doing the whole sober thing?"

My hands itch to smack the half-grin off his face, but I crumple the empty water bottle between them instead. "I don't have much of a choice. You know what that shit did to me and what it cost me. It's not anywhere I ever want to go back to."

Those few months before and just after I was discharged are nothing but a blur of bad decisions and hangovers. It wasn't pretty, and they both know it since they were the people who helped pull me from the bottom of the bottle— but not before I lost my spot on Delta and got medically discharged due to "mental health."

Still, I know they'd enjoy a cold one after traveling here. I grab them each a bottle of water and set them in front of them. It's the least I can do.

Chaos rolls it between his hands. "So, who's the girl?"

I glance at the door to ensure it's still closed and rest my palms on the granite, leaning forward slightly. "Detective Viktoria Garin of the NYPD."

They both raise their eyebrows.

Chaos snorts. "Then I'm even more interested in why you wanted us here. Considering any reason I can think of consists of things you don't want the fuzz knowing about."

I sigh and run a hand back through my damp hair. "She and her partner, Hank Grayson, were looking into the Russians and the same human trafficking ring. We bumped into each other at a club called B66. Turns out, this guy, Michail Yankovich, is holding monthly auctions for these girls."

Mouth's lips twist into a sneer, and Chaos clenches the water bottle tight enough that his knuckles whiten.

"Fucker."

"I share the sentiments. Anyway, while I was meeting with Grayson off the books to exchange information to try to advance either of our investigations, we got shot at."

Both of their eyes widen. Since all of our discharges, we've been dabbling in various endeavors that often require us to use the skills we were taught by Uncle Sam, but rarely are we dodging bullets anymore.

Chaos shakes his head. "Who was dumb enough to shoot at you?"

"The Russians. At least, I'm pretty sure it was them. Only, Grayson and I weren't the targets." I incline my head toward the bedroom. "She was."

"What?" Chaos stops fiddling with his bottle of water and raises an eyebrow at me. "Why?"

I release a deep sigh, the annoyance at finding out the information from Vik returning. "Apparently, she grew up in Brighton Beach, where there's a huge Russian population and thinks she was recognized at B66. Anyway, she got hit, but her partner had a buddy's girl patch her up. Then someone tried to nab her off the street, and I brought her here to keep her safe. And well..."

Chaos chuckles deeply. "You thought your dick would keep her safe?"

Asshole.

I chuck the empty water bottle at him, and he ducks to avoid it hitting his head. "Shut up, fucker. Show her some respect."

"Oh..." He holds up his hand. "Respect? Damn, you are really twisted up about this girl."

"Fuck you, man."

The last thing I want to be discussing with Chaos and Mouth is my situation with Vik. It's complicated enough without them tossing in their two cents when they know absolutely nothing about her and could never understand how easily she gets under my skin.

Chaos chugs half his water and smacks his lips. "So, what's the plan? What do you need us to do?"

I open my mouth to respond just as the door cracks and Viktoria peeks her head out. All eyes turn in her direction, and both Mouth and Chaos smirk.

This is going to be a shit-show.

The guys have never seen me with a woman—at least, not one who wasn't stripping on a pole. Giving each other shit is just part of our friendship, but when it comes to Vik, my protective instinct seems to go beyond keeping the Russians from putting more bullet holes in her.

Though, I can't keep her from the boys forever.

No matter how much I may want to.

I wave for her to join us, and she slips from the door into the loft and slowly makes her way over to the kitchen.

"Guys, this is Detective Viktoria Garin." I motion toward Chaos, who looks even worse than usual with his dark hair disheveled and blue eyes rimmed with dark circles from lack of sleep. "Viktoria, this is Kalen Riggs, but you can call him Chaos, and this is Jude Lawson"—I point toward the brick house with the haunting gaze that seems to bore right through anyone he looks at—"but he goes by Mouth."

They both incline their heads toward her in recognition, but neither says nor does anything else to acknowledge the fact that they just watched me fuck her in the shower.

Given how they arrived and the first impression they made, the need to defend them to Vik rises before I can stop it. "I trust these guys with my life, and you should, too."

She joins me on my side of the counter and offers them a tight smile. "Nice timing, boys."

I bark out a laugh that echoes around the loft space. Leave it to Vik to have a smartass comment after being caught in the act. "I was just about to fill the guys in on the plan. I scoped out the warehouses, and I've excluded a few where there were clearly no signs of anyone being there recently. But I haven't pinpointed it yet. The boys and I will do some more recon tomorrow and nail it down. Then I'll get a hold of Hank, and we can all meet and finalize the plan."

Based on what I saw, any of the warehouses should be fairly easy to get in and out of, but Yankovich's men are armed to the teeth wherever they are, so it won't come without a lot of bullets flying. That means this needs to be organized carefully, and I need Chaos and Mouth and Vik to all be on the same page.

The guys are rock solid. No questions there, but something tells me despite Vik's insistence, some reservations still linger—the kind that could get someone killed.

VIKTORIA

"Just what exactly *is* the plan? Besides getting the girls out of there."

Reaper exchanges a look with his friends and glances at me. "Am I giving you the law-enforcement-appropriate answer or the truth?"

His question makes acid rise up my throat, and I swallow it back and glance between the three men. If the other two are anything like Reaper—which I assume they are, or he wouldn't have asked them here to be involved in something like this—then they aren't going to hesitate to pull the trigger if necessary.

Even though I resigned myself to the fact that the vigi-lante-style of justice that will be happening might be neces-sary in these dire circumstances, and that getting the department involved would likely only complicate things in a way that could cost these women their lives, it doesn't mean the cop in me doesn't still feel a bit uneasy about all of it.

Still, I made my decision and laid all my cards on the table with Reaper. There isn't any way to go back now.

"The real answer. I have to know what to expect."

Reaper leans his hip against the counter, addressing me, scanning my face to see if I really mean it or if I'm just placating him. "If we arrest these guys, what are the chances of them actually getting convicted and doing any time? What are the chances that while they are in there, someone else doesn't just pick up the business?"

Pretty slim.

It's the unfortunate reality of the court system and the

power men like Yankovich have. Money and connections often mean justice isn't served and the perps walk. Frustrating for a cop who spends months or even years building a case and for the prosecutors, but even more so for the victims.

I just need to keep reminding myself who I'm doing this for—those innocent women and girls.

But Reaper doesn't wait for me to respond, clearly intending those to be rhetorical questions—or maybe because he's worried about what I'll say, especially in front of his friends.

"We need to take them out, Vik—each and every one of them. We need to make a statement that this type of trafficking isn't going to happen without repercussions. The only way to do that is to spill as much blood as possible." He pauses and narrows his eyes on me. "You have a problem with that?"

I look from him to his friends, waiting for one of them to show even an ounce of hesitance or guilt. "None of you do?"

A smile plays on Chaos' lips, but Mouth, who still hasn't said a thing, sits stoically on his stool, his elbows resting on the counter.

Well, I guess that answers that question.

Not that I expected anything different, but the fact that people can take lives so easily still unnerves me. I can't let it affect this situation, though.

I turn back to the man I just let destroy me in the shower, my body heating at the memory and with the returned embarrassment of knowing Chaos and Mouth witnessed at least the end of it. "I guess I can't expect anything else from a man called Reaper, can I?"

He crosses his arms over his chest and shakes his head. "Don't make the mistake of thinking I *like* doing this, that *any* of us get off on taking lives. Sometimes, it's just necessary, Vik." He glances at his friends. "Believe me, I had no idea what I was walking into when Cutter asked me to help take out the man responsible for his friend's girl being trafficked. I had no clue it would lead to all of this. But I couldn't just walk away then, and I can't walk away now with these guys still breathing. Not when the criminal justice system is so fucked up. Between payoffs and plea deals, some or all of these guys could end up walking, and then, where would we end up? With another warehouse full of girls."

Chaos leans back slightly. "But we don't know exactly where they are?"

Reaper returns his focus to him. "I found a source who said they were in a warehouse by the Jersey docks. Scoping it all out, I was able to exclude a bunch of them, but we have to do some additional recon, and of course, see if we can get the plans to the building. Then, we'll meet with Hank and the Satan's Knights in a couple days when we're ready."

"The Satan's Knights?" Chaos raises an eyebrow. "As in, the motorcycle club?"

I nod and release an annoyed sigh that draws a knowing look from Reaper.

He shakes his head and addresses Chaos. "Their involvement is a long story I'll tell you later. Just know we're all on the same side of this."

All on the same side.

I wish I could believe that was true. But it's hard to think of myself as being on the same side as criminals and vigilantes. Still, I guess that's where I am. Where I've chosen to be. Because, like it or not, the only reason I'm here is of my own choosing.

Of course, the alternative is to be locked inside that

room until this is all over, but I need to do good where I can when I can—even if it means eating away at my own conscience a little bit.

If Reaper and his friends think the only way to end this is putting a bullet or ten into the men behind it, then maybe they're right. They've spent their entire careers defending this country and innocent people against threats all over the world. I may not agree with their methods, but maybe I'll just have to learn to live with them.

Like I'll have to learn to live with what I've done with Reaper.

Involving myself emotionally with a man as cold as he is ruthless is just setting myself up to have my heart broken. Just like he'll pull the trigger on Yankovich, he's going to pull the trigger and end whatever this is between us when his mission is all said and done.

I'll be left to wonder what might've been if we had met under different circumstances or if I've made a huge mistake. To be haunted forever by the memories of his rough, calloused hands touching me, his warm lips pressed against the most intimate spots of my body, his tongue...

A shudder rolls through me, one I'll likely experience every day of my life going forward, remembering this time we had together.

Not the smartest move, Viktoria.

No, not at all.

17

VIKTORIA

The Satan's Knights clubhouse looks a hell of a lot different when there are still hints of sunlight on the horizon and I'm not drunk on whiskey and in excruciating pain after being shot.

It isn't much of a clubhouse at all, really, just a dive bar that apparently allows them to use a room at the back. Not exactly what one expects when they picture the home of a one-percenter MC. Though, it isn't really my department, so while I was familiar with the group prior to our fateful meeting, I can't say I've ever really spent any time considering where they do their business. And when they dragged me here to patch me up and Hank brought me home after, I wasn't really concerned with where the makeshift surgery had occurred.

But now that we're here to meet with Hank and the Satan's Knights to plan what could very well be a raid that ends my career as a cop, I can't help but feel the guilt, knowing I've gotten involved with these guys.

Their reputation precedes them, and now, I'm entering the lion's den, with three mercenaries hot on my heels—one of whom I'm sleeping with. Or more like fucking and getting very little sleep with.

Christ, how did you get in this situation, Vik?

Each step feels like marching toward my doom. Likely because the former president, Jack Parrish, stands at the end of the long, narrow hallway in front of an open door and motions for us to step inside.

Reaper urges me forward with a warm hand firmly at my lower back, and somehow, despite all the reasons it shouldn't, his touch there is like an anchor keeping me grounded in this moment and instead of overthinking everything like I want to.

And it's a good thing, too, because if I did truly stop to think about what we're about to do in this backroom, I would probably turn the other way and walk right out of here.

As it stands, it's only Reaper's physical presence at my back that keeps me moving forward in the room that isn't at all what I expected. Several tables from the bar have been pushed together to form one long one in the center, and Satan's Knight's insignia occupy all the wall space. But it isn't nearly as intimidating as I anticipated. Maybe I've mentally psyched myself out for no reason whatsoever.

Then my eyes fall on the man at the head of the table. His cut says "*WOLF*" and bears the patch reading "*President.*" He must be the man who took over from Parrish when he stepped down...and he doesn't look too pleased with this meeting.

Reaper leans in and brushes his lips against my ear. "Just stay cool, Vik."

Stay cool?

I shoot him a dirty glare over my shoulder, but he just grins and urges me toward an empty seat on the near side of the table. Parrish motions for us to sit, and Chaos and Mouth drop into seats on the other side of Reaper while the rest of the Satan's Knights settle into the other empty chairs, leaving only one open and one very important person missing from this meeting.

"Where's Hank?"

Almost as if on cue, he hustles through the door, looking slightly disheveled and exasperated. "Hey, sorry I'm late." His eyes land on me, and he sighs in relief. "Vik, are you all right?"

The look he casts at Reaper tells me he hasn't been all that comfortable with the situation despite his conversations with the man and likely has a thousand questions I'm not sure I want to answer about what's been happening while I've been with our mercenary friend.

I glance around the room at all the hard eyes watching us and nod. "I'm good. We'll talk later."

Hank seems to catch the drift and settles into the empty chair on the opposite side of the table.

Parrish leans forward in his chair and rests his elbows on the table. "Now that we're all here, let me introduce you to Wolf, our current prez."

Wolf inclines his head toward each of us, a snarl on his lips. "Let me be clear; I don't take kindly to being kept in the dark about shit like this." He turns his beady eyes on Parrish and fixes him with a glare. "Getting in deep with cops and mercenaries is not how this club operates anymore."

Parrish rolls his eyes. "If this is the part where we whip out our dicks to see who the bigger man is here, I feel I should remind you there is a lady in the room." He spits out his toothpick and crosses his arms against his chest.

"We all get it, brother; you're in charge. But Yankovich is personal."

"Damn straight he is, but that isn't exclusive to you. The Yankovich family has inflicted pain on everyone with a fucking patch. Need I remind you, who shot my son while you had me tied to a fucking chair?"

"Pop," the guy with the patch that reads *"NICO"* calls from across the table. "Not the time."

"Yeah, Scotto," Parrish interjects. "That's old fucking news. The Satan's Knights involvement in this operation is justified no matter how you spin it."

Hank clears his throat. "With all due respect, can you two handle this after we get the girls to safety because time is not on our side?"

Wolf regards Hank with a look. "Our club is at your disposal. Whatever resources you need—men, ammo, a place to crash while this is all going on—it's all yours."

Parrish uncrosses his arms and slaps his palms against the table. "Great, now can we get the fuck on with it? What's the plan?"

Reaper shifts next to me and leans forward. "I've located the warehouse where they're holding the girls. Chaos, Mouth, and I sat on it all day yesterday, and we have a good feeling of their schedules and what we can expect going in when it comes to resistance. We also grabbed the blueprints that were filed with the city when it was built, so we have a good idea of the internal layout and structure. What we don't know is how many girls there are or how much help we'll need getting them out of there."

Hank shifts uneasily in his seat, his gaze darting from Parrish and over to us. "That's going to be a problem."

Reaper raises an eyebrow at him. "Why is that?"

"We have to get Anastasia and the kids to safety. If we go

in for the girls and Yankovich somehow gets wind of that, all he has to do is call the guard he has watching her and she's done."

Parrish leans forward. "Yeah, and if we get her and the kids out first, he's going to lock that warehouse down tight. He might even move the girls before we can get them. We're fucked either way."

Shit.

While this Anastasia woman has tried to assist us since Hank first made contact, I never thought about the fact that we'd have to worry about her, too, when the bullets started flying.

With an annoyed sigh, Reaper leans back in his chair and shrugs. "We hit them both at the same time. You and the Knights get Anastasia and the kids, and Chaos, Mouth, and I will go into the warehouse."

Oh, hell no!

"You, Chaos, Mouth, and *me*." I lean forward and turn until my gaze meets his. "Don't think you're leaving me out of this raid, Reaper."

The corner of his mouth twitches. "I wouldn't dream of it. If we hit them both at the same time, no one can issue a warning. We should have a chance of getting everyone out safely."

A chance...

Those words don't instill a lot of confidence. Unease coils and tightens around my spine, making me shift uncomfortably in my seat.

Hank apparently shares my worry. "Are you going to be able to do it with just four of you?"

Reaper exchanges a look with his buddies. "We've handled worse."

Somehow, I don't doubt that. I've seen the evidence of it

permanently marked across his skin and in the way his buddies' eyes constantly dart around the room, taking in every detail and missing nothing.

Still, it seems like a tall order for the four of us to take on potentially dozens of men at the warehouse alone, even if we do have the best-trained men in the country on our side.

There has to be more we can do. More *I* can offer to this mission.

"What if we stack the deck in our favor?"

All eyes in the room turn to me.

Hank shifts in his seat and narrows his gaze on me. "What do you mean?"

"Well..." I cast a hesitant peek at Reaper, who has gone stock still next to me. "We suspect I was the target of the shooting, right?"

Everyone nods their agreement.

I swallow and avoid looking at Reaper when I finally lay out my plan. "So, we know they would be interested if I showed up at the warehouse, right? Maybe I should draw them out of the building. It makes them easier targets if they're out in the open on the docks."

REAPER

"Are you fucking *insane?*" I don't bother trying to hide the anger from my voice. Even if I had made an attempt to, I would have failed. Miserably. As it stands now, I wouldn't be surprised if steam were coming out of my ears like in the old cartoons as I stare at Viktoria. "You *must* be completely unhinged if you think there's any way in *hell* I'm going to let you be *bait* for the guys who tried to *kill* you once already."

How can she even suggest *such absolute lunacy?*

Fisting my hands on the top of the table, I wait for her to offer some sort of explanation for her crazy, ridiculous, absolutely stupid suggestion.

Hank snorts from his place across the table and holds up his hand to point at me. "I actually agree with Dixon. That's not happening."

Viktoria has the nerve to look shocked by our reactions. "What? Why not? We know they want me."

I slam my fist onto the table, making several people twitch in their seats. Maybe an unwise move around these guys. "Because I'm not going to put your life at risk *again* any more than we have to."

Hank clears his throat. "Neither am I, Vik. I'm the one who dragged you into this. I'm the reason you got shot and you're risking your badge. I'm not going to let you be bait for a madman, too."

At least Hank and I are in agreement with this insanity. If he backed her idea, we might have a very serious and bloody problem on our hands. As it stands now, Vik will undoubtedly tear into me at the first chance she gets once we're somewhere private. But I can handle her, especially when I have her partner backing me—along with everyone else in the room, which I have to assume is true since no one is jumping in to say her plan has any merit.

Vik scowls and glances from Hank to me, shooting daggers at both of us with hard eyes, her arms crossed over her chest. "I'm a big girl and capable of making my own decisions on this."

I slide my hand onto her leg and squeeze her thigh as I lean in. What I'm about to say isn't for everyone's ears. "We had a deal, Vik. You would stay by my side or at my fucking six so I can keep an eye on you the entire time if I was going to let you out of that room. Your idea isn't the deal, and it isn't happening. End of fucking discussion."

Her mossy eyes lock with mine, defiance flashing in their depths.

Just fucking try me, Vik.

I won't think twice about tossing her over my shoulder again, throwing her right back into that room, and keeping her locked up until this is all over.

And it looks like she's more than ready to argue and fight this out. She opens her soft, pink lips to do it when Wolf bangs his meat mallet "gavel" against the table.

"I don't know what the fuck is going on with you guys, but if anyone gives a shit, I'm in agreement that it's best if we go in unannounced." He shakes his head and narrows his gaze at Parrish. "And this is why we don't do business with these types."

Chaos finally speaks up from beside me. "This is what we do best, guys. We can handle it." He cuts his gaze to Viktoria. "*Without* putting anyone at unnecessary risk."

Her entire body goes rigid, her leg stiffening under my palm, and I know what she wants to say—that all of this is an unnecessary risk—but she bites back her comment and settles in her chair, huffing and re-crossing her arms over her chest angrily.

Parrish chuckles from his spot across the table. "Well, since that's settled...it looks like we all have some more specific planning to do." He looks at Reaper. "You let us know if you guys want any additional men or resources."

Wolf shoots him a dirty look, but Parrish either doesn't see it or doesn't care. Whatever is going on with those two, I wouldn't want to be stuck in the middle of it. Nor do I anticipate needing any help from the Satan's Knights. After what Chaos, Mouth, and I saw when staking out the place,

I'm confident we can get in and out without too much trouble.

I nod and squeeze Vik's leg. "We'll be fine."

And I will have a *serious* conversation with Vik when we get back to the safehouse about the little plan she suggested. One she is definitely not going to enjoy.

Everyone pushes back from the table. I place my hand at Vik's back to steer her from the room, but she glances over her shoulder at me with a scowl and inclines her head toward Hank.

"I need to talk to my partner for a minute. *Alone.*"

Her brush-off shouldn't bother me. Hank has been her partner for a long time, and they had a relationship long before I was in the picture in any capacity. But still, the edges of my vision go green as she rounds the table and approaches him, dragging him to the far corner of the room where they can talk in private.

Is this what jealousy feels like?

It isn't anything I've ever experienced because I've never allowed myself to care enough about any one woman to give two shits about who or what she does when she isn't with me.

Hank wraps an arm around her shoulder, and I fist my hands at my sides to keep myself from crossing the room and doing something very unwise to Detective Grayson.

Chaos claps me on the shoulder. "You might want to wipe that sneer off your face if you want any chance of that woman ever letting you do what you did to her in the shower or what I heard you two doing the last few nights ever again."

Fucking asshole.

I turn toward him and flip him off. "Fuck you, Chaos. What the hell would *you* know about how to deal with a woman, anyway? Didn't your ex-wife leave your ass high and dry during your first deployment?"

Shit. Maybe that was going a bit too far.

He stills, and his lips press into a firm line as he leans in so the men lingering in the room can't hear whatever he's about to say—likely a good thing. "Don't pretend to know my personal business, Reaper. You don't have the first fucking clue about anything."

This isn't the time to delve into his complicated personal life, even though I stand by my assertion that he perhaps isn't the best person to be offering love life advice.

I shrug off his hand from my shoulder and turn toward the door. "You're right. My bad." I try to shake out the tension building in my shoulders, but another glance at Hank and Vik whispering in the corner only tightens my muscles even more. "I just want this whole thing over and done with."

Chaos raises an eyebrow at me, following my gaze. "What? The raid or your time with Viktoria?"

Fuck if I know.

And that's the entire problem.

18

REAPER

The cool breeze off Newark Bay flutters Vik's hair around her where she crouches down next to me, gun in hand, eyes laser-focused on the warehouse in front of us. Despite the river being right there, that damn scent of summer flowers invades my breath, tightening my hand on my weapon.

How the hell can she still smell like that when she doesn't have her things at the safe house?

It's just how she smells, and it's fucking with my head in ways we can't afford right now.

Leaning into her only makes it worse, but I can't risk being heard. I brush my lips against her ear. "I told you to put your fucking hair up."

Vik turns her head toward me until our lips almost brush. "And I told you to fuck off."

I grab her upper arm and drag her chest up against mine. "We don't need any distractions, including your goddamn hair tickling me in the fucking wind."

Even though it isn't in Vik's nature not to argue back, she relaxes slightly and inclines her head toward mine in acknowledgment. "You could've just fucking said that."

She hands me her gun, quickly pulls up her hair into a messy bun with a hair tie around her wrist, then settles back in next to me and holds out her open palm. I slap the gun into it with an annoyed glare at her before I return my focus to the warehouse.

The big, dark-blue conversion van they use to deliver late-night food to Yankovich's men every night since we started watching the place pulled in a few minutes ago, and the food was unloaded and brought inside quickly. Now, all we have to do is wait for the agreed-upon signal to go in.

Viktoria shifts next to me. "You really think this is the right time to go in?" She glances at me with concerned eyes. "We shouldn't wait 'til there are fewer men inside?"

It isn't the first time she's expressed her concern with the plan Chaos, Mouth, and I came up with. She wanted to go in while the two guys who always grab the food were gone, but we shot down that idea pretty damn fast.

I shake my head and lean into her again. "Like I told you before, when they're eating, they're not going to be paying attention. Ten distracted men are better than eight men on full alert."

She nods her understanding and shifts in her squat again, though whether she's uncomfortable in the position or her nerves are getting to her remains unclear.

I scan the entire area around us, focus moving from building to building and the quiet docks that are basically empty this time of night. What we're about to do could draw a lot of unwanted attention, and there's a good chance one or all of us may end up in cuffs on the way out of here. But it'll be worth it if the girls are safe. Whether because we set them free or because the cops show up at the sound of gunfire and intervene.

The former would be preferred, but either way, this might be the last moment I get alone with Viktoria—maybe ever. I didn't want to think about it last night when she straddled me and slowly rode up and down on my cock. I didn't want to think about it when she leaned down and kissed me, her dark hair falling around us like curtains against the world outside, keeping us in that moment just a little longer so we could pretend that the private world we have been living in wasn't coming to an end the next day.

Not thinking about it allowed us to ignore what we did over and over and over again until we both collapsed so exhausted we could barely move then wrapped around each other. It allowed me to keep ignoring the reality of what tonight would bring.

It was the best damn night's sleep I've ever had in my entire life. In the arms of a woman who simultaneously makes me want to strangle her and kiss her senseless. A woman who hates everything I stand for and stands for everything I believe in. A woman who's ready to go into that warehouse with us, guns blazing, to rescue innocent women and ensure that they're safe, even if it costs her the badge she's worked her entire life for.

I glance at her out of the corner of my eye. "Be careful, Vik. Remember, stay with me at all times—at my side or on my six."

She opens her mouth to say something but then quickly presses her lips together and nods. It's too late for any further reservations or concerns. We're too far in to go back now. We don't have time to scrap tonight and regroup. Not with the auction coming up so fast.

It's now or never.

The light over the dock door where they pulled up the van goes out, a sign they've finished bringing in all the food and won't be back outside the rest of the night unless something draws them out. It's also our signal to go in.

If all goes as planned, they'll be so distracted eating that they won't know what hit them until it's too late for them to respond and formulate any sort of counterattack.

What I said in that meeting yesterday was true. Chaos, Mouth, and I have seen shit and faced odds a lot worse than this. I'm not worried about us, though. I'm worried about those women and Vik. One stray bullet is all it takes to end the life of somebody who doesn't deserve it instead of the bad guys. Which is why we're going to be careful and stick to the plan.

I raise my hand and signal to Vik that we're moving. She sends off a text to Hank to let them know to move that just says "now," then we dodge out from around the buoys where we've been taking cover at the side of the dock and make our way through the shadows toward the warehouse where the Russians are holding the girls.

Vik stays directly behind me, her soft footsteps barely audible to anyone but me. But even if I couldn't hear her, I would feel her. Whenever that woman is within a hundred feet of me, my heart races, and my body responds.

It's more dangerous to both of us than whatever lies inside this building. Yet, I can't bring myself to regret anything that's happened since the day I met her in that club. Not when I have felt things with her that I never thought possible. It's why having her with us tonight ups the stakes so much. Because it isn't just about rescuing these girls and making sure the fuckers pay for their sins; it also means protecting this woman to ensure that when this is all said and done, she still has her life and her job.

God willing...

If I still believed in the big man upstairs, I might actually send up another prayer for what we're about to do, but my faith in a higher power died a long time ago with my friends on a sandy road across the fucking world. It didn't help them, and it didn't keep Vik from leaving her apartment the other day, either.

We reach the side of the building and duck into the shadowy recesses of a side door. While Vik keeps her eyes on what's happening behind us, I quickly pick the lock. These idiots didn't even upgrade the security doors on this place. They're so fucking confident no one would ever come at Yankovich that they've gotten complacent.

That just makes things easier for us.

Hopefully...

According to the blueprints we found for the building, this door leads to a small hallway filled mostly with janitorial closets and other small storage. There shouldn't be any reason for any of Yankovich's men to be back here. More than likely, they'll be in the kitchen or doing God knows what with the girls, who we assume are being held somewhere in the main warehouse area.

I would've loved to have gotten eyes inside somehow before we came in tonight, but we had to work with what's available. Which isn't much. Still, with Chaos, Mouth, and Vik with me, I'm confident we can get these girls out of here safely.

As long as all goes as planned. And unfortunately, one thing my time in Delta taught me is that even the best-laid plans can go to shit in an instant.

Tightening my grip on my weapon, I ease open the door, listening for any noise on the other side, but all remains quiet. Only the sound of Vik's soft breathing behind me fills my ears.

I signal for her to follow me, and the determined look she shoots encourages me that she is one hundred percent on her game. Her bullet wound has healed well, and any lingering pain from it seems to be a long-forgotten memory.

Just like I'll be once this is over and I leave.

But I can't get ahead of myself. It's essential to stay in the moment when we have such an important job to do first.

The dark hallway in front of us might seem ominous to some, but it gives us the cover of darkness to enter the building. We make our way in, pausing at each door and clearing several small storage rooms. Chaos and Mouth will enter from the opposite side and meet us at the rendezvous location, assuming no one runs into any resistance before then. And the sound of laughter trickling down the hallway seems to suggest we won't.

Our plan is to hit them when their guard is down and they're concentrating on something else, like eating, and it seems as though we correctly assessed the situation. Nothing hints at them being aware we've breached the warehouse walls and are almost on them.

They have no idea what's coming, and once we unleash it on them, there won't be any escape from our wrath.

I pause a few feet from the open door to the kitchen, light and voices pouring out to the dark hall. Viktoria stops behind me, the warmth of her body radiating against my side, reminding me she's safe—at least for the moment.

Chaos and Mouth approach stealthily from the opposite direction and pause just on the other side of the door, weapons at the ready.

Here we go.

I hold up three fingers and take one deep breath before starting the silent countdown.

Three...

Two...

One...

VIKTORIA

Three...

Blood rushes loudly in my ears, like waves crashing against the shore, while watching Reaper start the countdown. Everything around me moves almost in slow motion. Three fingers. Then another one slowly goes down. I hold my breath, my own inhalations sounding almost deafening with us trying to be so silent.

All my senses are heightened. The scent of something spicy reaches my nose from inside the kitchen. The chill in the air raises goosebumps across my exposed arms.

Two...

Reaper's eyes flick over to meet mine, and I get lost for what feels like forever swimming in the sea blue. Then he returns his focus to the door and lowers the second finger.

One...

He closes his hand.

It's go time.

Reaper and Chaos both turn to face the door and begin firing. This isn't a mission to take prisoners or ensure we'll be able to question anyone. They have one goal—take out anyone who stands in the way of us freeing those girls, at any cost.

Excited yells in Russian fill the air, mingling with gunfire

exploding all around us, too muffled for me to make out
what they're saying. Reaper and Chaos move into the room,
leaving Mouth and me at the door. The silent but clearly
deadly man moves in immediately after them, weapon blazing, and I take my position just inside the jamb to watch the
hallway and ensure no one else is coming to join the melee.

Heavy footsteps come from my left, and the moment
Yankovich's man turns the corner, I unleash on him, firing
three shots straight to his chest. He drops before he even has
a chance to pull his weapon, and I glance over my shoulder
to take in what's happening behind me in the small kitchen.

The shots have stopped, and Reaper, Mouth, and Chaos
appear to be checking the bodies of the men down on the
peeling linoleum floor. Blood pools under them, and the
splashes of it across the already dingy walls adds another
dash of evidence of the pure violence that has been
unleashed in the room.

These guys decimated them. Took out what appears to
be seven men in less than thirty seconds. And watching the
way they work—so precise, so skilled, no reservations—
sends a little shiver of appreciation through my body that I
never thought I'd feel.

Reaper is a killer. A man trained to be absolutely lethal
and one who takes his job seriously. A man who carries out
his work easily, without a second thought.

Knowing it's true and witnessing it in person are two
different things. While I probably should be more worried
about the ramifications of what they've just done, instead, a
sense of pride blooms in my chest at how fucking badass
Reaper really is.

Mouth collects weapons from the bodies, and Reaper
pushes up from the squat he was in over one of the bodies
and turns toward me, his jaw hard.

"Yankovich isn't here. Neither is Kosofik."

I glance up and down the hallway. "You think either of them is in the building?"

Reaper approaches with Chaos and Mouth directly behind. "Kosofik was here last night when we came after our meeting at the Knights' clubhouse. And he was here the night before."

"Maybe he just hasn't come yet?"

Chaos offers a half shrug. "It's possible, or he might be tied up somewhere else tonight."

A low growl rumbles in Reaper's chest. "I was hoping we could take out that fucker here. But let's keep moving. We need to find the girls."

The reminder of our mission replaces that tiny sense of dread, and Reaper pushes past me out the hallway to the left. I follow behind him without even thinking about it, his command to stay with him still blaring through my head.

Even last night, as he gripped my wrists together above my head in one of his large, calloused hands while he drove into me slowly, almost sweetly, he reminded me of our deal. Of the fact that I would never leave his side.

I wondered then, and I still wonder now, whether he strictly means that in terms of today or if there was some broader hidden meaning to his words that neither one of us were ready to consider last night—or maybe *anytime* in the near future.

God knows I'm not.

Making our way toward the end of the hallway that splits off in two directions isn't the time to do it, either. Reaper signals for Mouth and Chaos to go right, and I follow him to the left, down a long, poorly illuminated hallway. One of the neon lights that is actually lit flickers randomly, casting our path in an eerie and ominous glow.

After the explosive gunfire in close quarters, the strange silence surrounding us leaves my heartbeat flooding in my ears, the only sound besides our soft footsteps.

It's unlikely anyone outside heard the shots, though. This portion of the docks is largely quiet and unused this time of night, and when the boys scoped out the other warehouses, the vast majority of them were dust-covered and empty, unused for a while.

But one thing being a cop for all these years has taught me is to never make assumptions. That's the kind of thing that gets you killed. If the girls are here, they should have heard the shots. There isn't any way to hide that kind of carnage. They're likely hiding and terrified, unsure of what's happening. Just like we could be rescuers, we could just as easily be someone even worse than Yankovich's men attacking the facility to get their hands on them.

I try to put myself in those women's shoes, to consider what I might be thinking if I were trapped here in this moment, locked up and likely restrained for God knows how long—potentially months or years if they've been brought from elsewhere like most are. The thought raises bile in my throat, and I swallow it down as we reach the jamb of a cracked door to our left.

Reaper pauses and signals to go in and clear it. He pushes it open all the way, and we step into a small, dark office with an old metal desk and ripped leather chair occupying one corner. Papers litter the desktop, some words in English jumping out, but most of it in Russian.

He motions for me to watch the door while he approaches the desk and shifts around some of the papers until his eyes narrow. He grabs one and lifts it to read in the darkness of the room, only illuminated by the faint moonlight coming in from the solitary window on the far wall.

"What is it?" I ask the question as quietly as possible, but it still sounds deafening after the silence of making our way down here.

He approaches and holds it up for me to see. "A list. I assume of everyone who should be here." He swallows thickly, his hard gaze cutting over to me. "And prices they want to start the bidding at."

"Shit." I check the hallway again, tension tightening my back. Even though Reaper held that "menu" in his hand, seeing a version of it for myself makes our mission even more urgent.

"Let's move." Reaper brushes past me through the door and then sweeps out, checking both directions down the hallway.

I follow him again, trying to match his pace while keeping my steps as light as possible, and we make our way toward where the blueprints said the main warehouse would be. Though, any number of changes could've been made to the building since it was first constructed decades ago. The plans gave us a nice basis to go on but expecting the unexpected is all part of a mission like this.

The closer we move down the hallway toward the warehouse, the thicker the crackle of energy in the air grows, making the hair on my arms raise.

I don't like this.

It's not often my gut warns me to back away or turn around, but every nerve in my body screams at me to get the fuck out of here right now. That isn't an option, though.

I shake my head to try to clear it and stop behind Reaper at the opening of one of the doors to what should lead to the warehouse. Reaper glances back at me, his hard blue eyes sharp as ice.

It looks like he wants to say something, but he remains

frozen, looking at me for what feels like forever, though it's likely only a few moments, before he gives me a simple nod and then turns.

The sound of the gunshots comes so fast, I don't even have time to react to it, and Reaper crumples to the floor in front of me.

19

VIKTORIA

N*o!*

All the air whooshes from my lungs, my breath stalling as my chest tightens.

No. No. No!

I turn the corner the rest of the way, stepping over Reaper's legs, gun ready to nail whatever fucker shot Reaper, but instead of unleashing a torrent of bullets, I freeze with my finger on the trigger.

Oh, my God...

Row after row of metal-framed beds fill the entire interior of the dimly lit warehouse, dozens, maybe a hundred of them, and too many terrified eyes to count watch me from the gloomy darkness. Metal chains glint in what little light the failing overhead lamps provide, leading from the frames to frail wrists and ankles of more women than we ever anticipated.

It's worse than we could have ever imagined. Far more women on a much larger scale than we planned for. There might be a hundred women and young girls here, maybe more. All frightened. Maybe one armed.

Is it possible one of them somehow got a weapon from one of their captors and used it against Reaper, assuming he was one of Yankovich's men entering?

No matter how far I try to gaze into the gloom, I can't locate a weapon or anyone who could have possibly taken a shot at Reaper. Either one of these women has a gun, or the person who does is using the sea of trafficking victims as an opportune hiding place.

My skin pebbles with anticipation of something. Anything. I scan the room the best I can, keeping my eye on them as I kneel beside Reaper's prone body. Flat on his stomach, his face turned toward me, blood starts to pool out from under him, thick and red.

No. No. No. This can't be happening. This isn't the plan.
We didn't get this far just to have it end like this.

Gunfire sounds from somewhere else in the building, behind me and to the right, which means Chaos and Mouth are tied up elsewhere and won't be coming to give me any backup—at least, not in the immediate future.

I need to handle what's happening here on my own.

Pull your shit together, Vik.

This isn't any time to let nerves get the better of me. Not when Reaper's life and the lives of all these girls are at stake. I reach out with my free hand, check his pulse at his neck, and release a sigh of relief.

It's low and thready...but still there. That means there's hope. As long as I can get the bleeding to stop, he might have a chance. But it's impossible to focus on saving his life when I don't know who is threatening it or mine.

Keeping my eyes on the warehouse, I nudge Reaper's shoulder. "Reaper."

Instead of his usual smartass and growled response, I get nothing. And the room remains silent. No one moves or says a thing. In the dim lighting, it's hard to make out everything, and my gut clenches at the thought of the danger lurking in the shadows.

Still, I can't wildly shoot at what I can't see. If I hit any of those girls, I would never forgive myself. Not after everything we went through to get here and save them. Not after everything *they've* been through waiting for someone, *anyone,* to do the right thing and release them.

But the job is far from done. And I need the man lying at my feet as much as I need to take my next breath.

Please wake up. Please!

I shake Reaper again, harder, with more force than I probably need to or should use, but desperate times call for desperate measures. No movement or reaction.

Fuck you, Reaper. Don't leave me like this!

I pull my hand back and smack his cheek facing me, and this time, he sucks in a harsh breath and groans, wincing.

Thank fuck.

I push on his shoulder and roll him onto his back so I can better assess his injury while trying to keep one eye on the warehouse. He grits his teeth, pressing his right hand against the growing wound in his left shoulder.

Two inches to the right, and he would have taken the shot straight to the heart. Whether he moved at the last minute or whoever pulled the trigger just has shitty aim, either way, it probably saved his life. But he's still losing a lot of blood, and if we stay here much longer, he won't walk out of here at all.

"Get up, Reaper." I glance down at him, and his eyes flicker open but move, unfocused. "Get up!"

This time, my sharp order echoes through the space,

louder than I had intended it. Something shifts in the darkness to my left, but before I can turn, the cold muzzle of a gun presses to my temple.

Shit.

"Viktoria Garin..." Kosofik's heavily accented voice floats through the still, humid air of the warehouse and sends a chill down my spine. "To your feet." He presses the muzzle harder against my temple. "But you leave your weapon on the floor."

Shit. Shit. Shit.

I chance a glance at Reaper again. With his eyes closed, he appears to have fallen unconscious again, which means I'm on my own.

Fucking hell.

Slowly, I set my gun on the ground and push to my feet, then turn to face Kosofik, the barrel of his gun now pointed directly at my chest. The corner of his lips twitches, and he motions for me to move away from my weapon. I take two steps toward him, and he scans the room behind him briefly before returning his focus to me.

"I would say I'm impressed you finally located this place if I weren't so angry you succeeded in breaching it." Hard dark eyes meet mine. "My men let down their guard. But if I had been with them instead of in here checking on the girls, you never would've made it this far."

I fist my hands at my sides hard enough to make my nails bite into my palms. "But we *did*."

He glances down at Reaper bleeding on the cold gray concrete and smirks. "A lot of good that did you and your friend who calls himself...what was it? Adam Jones? I'll admit, I believed him for a moment. And I likely would have given him the location for our auction in a few days had you not moved in. He's a true professional. You"—he raises an eyebrow—"on the other hand. The fact that you thought you could walk into B66 and not be recognized just shows the arrogance you share with your brothers in blue."

"We don't know each other." I hold up my hands in hopes that it might convince him I'm willing to give up, even though that's the furthest thing from my mind. "You had already moved well beyond the neighborhood by the time I was born, so I know you weren't the one who recognized me."

He chuckles and shakes his head. "No. The girls are very loyal. Inessa recognized you immediately and alerted us within five minutes of you and your partner stepping into the club. From there, it was only a matter of keeping an eye on you to ensure you didn't interfere with what we had coming up." He offers me a smile that *almost* borders on kind. "I'll admit I never anticipated you getting this far or this close." He glances down at Reaper's body, unmoved, and I follow his line of sight. "But whoever your friend is clearly has skills you don't."

No doubt Anya could've located this warehouse just as easily as Reaper did with brute force, using her considerable hacking skills, but I had no intention of dragging her deeper into this than I already did by asking her to look into Reaper's background. And I'm not about to let Kosofik know about her involvement because if he knows who I am, then he knows I have a sister.

"Just what did you hope to accomplish here, Viktoria?" He raises a dark eyebrow and swings his free hand out toward the sea of women around him. "Did you think that you would actually get past all of us and free them? Did you think you would kill me?"

Anger tightens my fists as I lower them to my sides, suddenly unconcerned about whether he thinks I'm compliant or not. I'd rather go down fighting than go down giving up. "I thought maybe we could save them from this horrible life you forced them into."

He barks out a cynical, evil-sounding laugh that echoes around the place, making several of the women cower further behind the beds they're strung to. "Rescue them? From what? From men who would give them roofs over their heads, who would offer them food, shelter, and some even the chance to become life partners in a way most of these women could never even dream of. That's what *you're* trying to take away from them."

"Are you really so twisted and demented that you don't understand this is all in your fucking head? These women didn't choose this. They don't want to be slaves to grown men who have nothing better to do with their money than to buy humans. These women had lives. They had families, and you ripped them from them."

An evil grin twists his lips as he eyes me. "Maybe that's true. But it's too late to stop me. And despite what will undoubtedly be your initial reluctance, I have a specific client in mind who I'm sure can break you, given enough time."

REAPER

The world returns in a rush, slamming into me with gut-turning pain and a voice I hoped I would never hear again.

"But it's too late to stop me. And despite what will undoubtedly be your initial reluctance, I have a specific client in mind who I'm sure can break you, given enough time."

Fucking Kosofik.

He was here, lurking in the shadows, waiting for an opportunity.

"I will never break, Kosofik. You have such a low view of women, of what they can accomplish and what they deserve, that you underestimate me. And underestimate *them*." Viktoria's anger hangs on every word.

He chuckles, a low, deep sound that makes me want to leap up from the floor and pound him into it with my bare fists, but the screaming agony in my shoulder and the fact that he undoubtedly has a weapon aimed at Viktoria right now keeps me prone.

Kosofik isn't the type of man anyone should fuck with, yet Viktoria seems intent on aggravating him until he finally snaps and unloads on her.

"I don't underestimate you, Detective Garin. I have a very clear view of what you can accomplish. Which is nothing. You standing here without a weapon with your associate dead on the floor beside you with no way to escape...you've lost."

"*Have* I?"

Oh, hell. I know that voice.

The indignation. It's the same she's shown me since the moment I met her. It could get her fucking killed.

She shifts where she stands only a foot from me, the movement sending her scent wafting over me. "Our gunshots are sure to have alerted someone to what's happening here, and I've already called in the cavalry. The entire NYPD will rain down on this place so hard in the next minute that you won't know what hit you. You'll wish you stayed back in Russia rather than setting foot here, thinking you could pick up doing the dirty work you did there so easily."

He barks out another laugh that echoes around the warehouse that I only got a glimpse of before he hit me with that bullet.

But why didn't he take out Viktoria the moment she rounded the door?

"You're lying, Detective Garin. The NYPD has no idea what you're up to. If they did, a SWAT team would have burst into this place and overwhelmed us with force a long time ago. Instead, you and your friend arrived alone, which tells me that you're also working alone outside the law." He chuckles. "I guess it shouldn't surprise me for a girl from Brighton Beach. No matter what anybody does to try to escape it, it's inevitable."

"Fuck you, Kosofik."

That's my girl.

Pride swells in my chest to join the pain there, and I risk a quick glance to my side to assess the situation, barely opening my eyes enough to see a sliver. A mere foot from me, Viktoria stands tall, her shoulders back, eyes focused on the enemy where he stands in front of her. But he's alone. The only one of his crew left. I have no fucking clue where Chaos and Mouth went, but at least I know Kosofik's by himself. And that gives us the upper hand.

Watching through squinted, barely cracked eyes, I keep my focus on Kosofik and shift my hand, gritting my teeth at the pain moving my left arm causes, and curl my fingers around the back of Viktoria's ankle to let her know I'm awake and moving.

She freezes, going stock still. "I'll give you one more chance, Kosofik. Give me the weapon and surrender so I can set these poor women free."

His laughter booms around the warehouse again, along with the excited chatter of the women who must've overheard Viktoria. "You must be delusional, Detective Garin. All it would take is a flick of my finger against this trigger to end you. The only reason I haven't was because I needed to ensure that the NYPD wouldn't be coming. I've long suspected the NYPD is a bunch of useless assholes who think they're above the law because they pretend to enforce it. If you only knew how many of your men I have on my payroll, how many of them watch and wait and feed me all the information you have. I suspected the department knew nothing because I haven't heard anything, but you've just confirmed it for me, which means I no longer have any use for you. Except if I'm going to sell you."

"Over my dead fucking body."

Viktoria's rage vibrates through her words and into me, making adrenaline surge through my body. The weapon I was holding when I was hit lies to my right, and there isn't any way I can grab it without Kosofik noticing my movement. But the gun Viktoria laid on the ground sits a few inches from my left hand, and her body blocks most of mine.

I'll only have one chance at this. One opportunity and one shot before Kosofik unleashes his own. If I fuck it up, I'll lose her and bleed to death on this cold, hard concrete floor while the victims of Yankovich's trafficking ring watch their only chance at freedom disappear.

I squeeze Viktoria's ankle three times.

Please, Vik, understand what I'm saying...

This will only work if we're on the same page completely —something the two of us have failed at repeatedly basically since the moment we met. Unless we were in bed.

Three...

Two...

One...

I grab the weapon from the ground as she dives to the side, and I fire, unloading the entire magazine in Kosofik's direction before the pain and blood loss finally suck me back down to the concrete and under to the familiar darkness.

20

REAPER

A familiar scent drags me from what feels like the deepest sleep I've ever been in—blooming flowers on a summer day. The rest of my senses come back to me slowly. A clattering, banging of metal from another room. The weight of a blanket over me and the soft brush of a hand against my cheek.

Where the fuck am I? And why does it feel like I got hit by a fucking truck?

I force open my heavy eyelids to a dimly lit room and blink them until they finally focus on a familiar ceiling. My room at the loft. Another soft brush of a hand on my face makes me turn my head toward it.

Viktoria sits in a chair beside my bed. "Welcome back."

"Shit. How long was I out?"

She glances at the clock on the nightstand and releases a heavy sigh. "About twelve hours, which doesn't surprise me after the blood you lost and the drugs Chaos and Mouth pumped into you."

I try to move and groan, the bone-deep pain in my shoulder keeping me down. But the agony and her words bring a barrage of memories to assault me. Memories broken by long blank periods. "What happened?"

Viktoria offers me a little half-smile. "You don't remember?"

No matter how hard I try to drag up what happened in that warehouse, all I get are bits and pieces. I shake my head and run my right hand over my face, rubbing at my sore eyes. "Not everything. The last thing I remember was you standing down Kosofik."

Her free hand tightens into a fist, and she pulls her palm from my cheek and runs that hand back through her dark, silky hair, releasing another waft of that scent that would make me weak in the knees if I were standing. But considering how I feel, I'm pretty sure I'd collapse onto the floor if I even attempted it right now.

She presses her lips together in a firm line, her anger clearly not abated. "That fucker." She shakes her head and inhales sharply. "After you squeezed my ankle, I dove out of the way and you emptied the magazine."

"And I killed him?"

Viktoria snorts and leans in. "No. You didn't. Three of your shots hit him, but that fucker was still breathing and on his knees, so I grabbed your gun from the other side of your body and put one straight into his fucking heart to ensure he would never do something like this again."

"Holy shit. You killed him?"

She brushes her lips over mine gently and then pulls back. "I did."

A war wages in my chest, between being proud of her and being terrified of what it means. I try to push myself into a sitting position and only manage to get up a couple of inches before I have to drop back down and grit my teeth. "You could've called it in, Vik. Gotten an ambulance there and maybe saved his life so he could be charged and put on trial."

Viktoria presses her lips together and considers me for a moment, turmoil turning her green eyes even darker. "I could have, but that would've meant exposing you, too."

She did it to protect me?

The reality of what that could mean slams into me harder than the bullet Kosofik shot did.

"And you're okay with that?"

She sighs and shakes her head, relaxing back in her chair slightly. "Honestly, I don't know. After I did it, I rushed to your side to try to stop the bleeding, and then Chaos and Mouth appeared. They pulled you out of there and brought you back here to patch you up. The bullet was through and through and didn't appear to hit anything important. You're lucky."

"No shit." I glance at the bandage over my shoulder and try to move it but instantly regret that decision when agony burns down my arm and the entire left side of my body. It's far from the first time I've been shot, but Chaos and Mouth know I wouldn't want any drugs beyond what they had to give me to dig around in there. So that means this time, waking up is a lot more painful than any other. "So, what happened after I passed out?"

She pushes to her feet and paces, the reality of reliving what happened making her antsy. "Once I was sure they were long gone with you, I called it in."

"What happened when the cops showed up?"

The look she casts me could melt ice, and she shakes her head. "I'm going to have a lot of explaining to do when I meet with my boss later today. I just told them that the warehouse was full of women who have been trafficked by the Russians and that they would find a lot of bodies inside."

"How are you going to explain all of that?"

One of her dark eyebrows raises in question. "You mean without ratting out you, Chaos, and Mouth?"

I feel like an asshole even thinking it, which is why I didn't ask, but she inclines her head.

"I get it. I do. And I'll figure it out."

"What about Hank and the Knights?"

"They got Anastasia out. That's all I know."

"What's the deal with Hank and that woman, anyway?"

She sighs and shakes her head. "I don't know. Hank gets overly invested in these things, and now there's a pretty woman involved. When I talked with him at the Knights' clubhouse the other night, he tried to blow it off as nothing, but I've known him a long time—there's definitely something he's not saying. I'll see Hank this afternoon at our meeting. I snuck away from the scene last night to come back here to you. It was chaotic enough that I could easily, but I need to have answers at this meeting, ones that are going to be hard to come up with."

The anxiety over what she's going to have to do practically vibrates through her and into me, and guilt climbs up my throat. There's only one choice here, one thing I can do.

"Give me to your boss."

"What?" She freezes and whirls back to face me.

"He'll never believe you did all that, took them all out alone. There were too many different guns, too many different trajectories, too many men for you to have done it solo. And you protecting us is going to cost you your job. So, give me to him...and save yourself since I couldn't fucking do it at that warehouse."

VIKTORIA

"Are you out of your ever-loving mind?"

Maybe I misheard him. I must have.

There's no way he just volunteered to throw himself on the pyre for me. He knows what would happen if the District Attorney or God forbid the United States Attorney found out a former Delta Force operative was killing people on US soil.

I drop onto the chair next to his bed and glare at him, hoping it's enough to burn the insanity out of him. "If I give you to my boss, you're going to end up in prison for a very long time, maybe forever."

He shakes his head, his blue eyes softening with an affection I wasn't so sure he was capable of. "I failed at that warehouse. Failed to protect you. I couldn't even take out Kosofik. And now, I'm lying here like a useless piece of shit and you're about to sacrifice yourself for me."

"Cut the woe is me fucking bullshit!" Anger rises in my blood, making me clench my fists at the side of the bed. "You were half fucking dead and still managed to shoot the guy three times before you passed out. I may have saved our lives by ending it, but you sure as hell started it."

He continues to glare at me, his frustration with the situation building as fast as my annoyance with his attitude.

"I was exactly where you are not long ago, so I know what it feels like to be in your shoes. You hate being weak. I get it because I do, too. But you need to take some time to recover from this, and I'm not going to let you do that in a prison cell."

He snarls at me and pushes himself up with his good

hand, grimacing but leaning toward me, a sneer on his lips. "You're not sacrificing yourself for me, Vik. I won't allow it."

"*Allow*?" I raise an eyebrow at him and snort. "You don't have a fucking choice, Reaper. This is *my* life, *my* career. And Hank and I will walk in there and tell our boss what he needs to hear. If I lose my badge because of it, so be it. Those girls are free now. I don't know what more I could ask for."

Except you.

I bite back those final words as I stare him down, waiting for him to continue to argue with me about it. But he can talk until he's blue in the face, and it won't change what's about to happen. I'm going to walk out of here and go to that meeting. I'm going to sit there with Hank and have to explain to Captain Miller what we did. And why. And I'll do it without naming names. That will no doubt bring IA breathing down my neck and cost me my badge, but so be it.

The future is uncertain in so many ways...and not only with my career. I don't know if Reaper will even be here when I get back. The man is trained to disappear like a ghost, vanish without a trace, and even shot up, something tells me he can still do it so quickly I wouldn't even see the dust he kicks up on his way out.

But I can't bring myself to tell him how much I don't want him to leave. How badly I want to crawl into this bed with him and just stay there.

Instead, I swallow back those words and press my lips to his harshly before I push on his chest. "Lie back down. Get some sleep. I'll be back...if I can."

I rise to my feet and walk to the door, intent on not looking back unless he asks me to stay, but his silence speaks volumes. Enough to make me pause at the doorway but keep my focus on the kitchen where Chaos and Mouth struggle to cook something for themselves.

They probably saved his life as much as I did, but those men are just as lethal as Reaper. Only he hasn't just killed hundreds of men, he's also destroyed my soul because I don't know how I'm ever supposed to be with anyone else when all I will do is compare them to that man lying in the bed behind me.

Stop, Vik.

This isn't the time to think about it. Not when I have such an important meeting. I force myself to walk out and close the door behind me, essentially sealing my fate with Roderick Reaper Dixon.

21

VIKTORIA

Now I know how the suspects I question must feel when we sit on the opposite side of those crappy tables in the interrogation rooms. I shift in my seat under Captain Miller's scrutinizing gaze and cast a glance at Hank, where he sits beside me in the hard, uncomfortable wooden chairs in front of the captain's desk.

The moment I entered the precinct, the captain unceremoniously ushered me into his office, where Hank was already waiting. Which means my partner and I haven't even had a chance to talk before the inquisition begins.

Finally, after what feels like hours of sitting with nothing but awkward, uncomfortable, heavy silence between us, the captain leans forward and rests his elbows on his desk, clasping his hands together. "I honestly don't even know what to say, Garin. I expect this kind of shit from Grayson, but from you?" His hard gaze cuts through me like a knife. "You went into a warehouse, knowing it was likely filled with Yankovich's armed men as well as dozens of potential trafficking victims without calling it in. Then after discharging a weapon and killing several men, you did call it in and then fled the damn scene and left all of us to pick up the pieces and wonder what the fuck happened."

He releases a heavy sigh and leans back.

"Then *this* guy shows up and walks in with Yankovich in cuffs and says he has the evidence we need to charge him."

"What?" I jerk upright in my seat and turn to Hank. "You arrested Yankovich?"

I never got any details of their portion of the mission other than a text that the woman and her kids were safe. Yankovich never came into the conversation.

Hank raises an eyebrow at me and clears his throat. "As I was just telling the captain, you didn't have any choice but to act. And I made it clear to you that you had to. There wasn't any time to wait for backup. The lives of all of those women depended on it. I explained that all of this was my fault. That I knew once I arrested Yankovich, word would get back to his men at the warehouse and they would likely kill the girls so that none of them could testify. I sent help for you, and you were completely unaware of the identities of the men who then left before the police arrived."

Oh, my God. What in the hell is he doing?

He's taking the fall for me.

Oh, oh God. No. No. No. No. No. No. No. No.

I open my mouth to object, to tell the captain that I knew exactly what I was doing and made the conscious choice to get involved, but Hank shoots out a hand and wraps it around my wrist.

"It's okay, Vik. I have to own up to what I did. Tell the captain the truth."

The hard look he offers me tells me exactly what he wants me to say. He wants me to cover my ass and go along with the story. He wants to take the fall completely, even if it costs him his badge.

Fuck. Fuck. Fuck. Fuck. Fuck.

I can't believe only a few days ago, I was questioning whether I could ever trust Hank again, and now, here he is, ready to fall on his sword even though I made a very conscious decision to help him, knowing the risks.

"I-I'm sorry, Captain, that I didn't phone it in right away. I happened to be in the area, right around the corner actually, and Hank knew I could get there fast."

Captain Miller raises his brows. "And you couldn't pick up the fucking radio and call it in?"

"I wasn't in a squad car. I didn't even have my gun on me since I've been on my little vacation. Hank said someone would meet me there to assist. I'm sorry. I didn't even get the guy's name."

Hank squares his shoulders. "And you're not going to, either, Captain. I'm perfectly prepared to face the ramifications of what I've done, but the people who helped me did so to save those poor girls. I'm not about to let them all go down for that when I can protect their identities."

Good God. He's really taking this all the way...

The captain releases another heavy sigh and leans back in his chair. "You'll likely be criminally charged." He cuts his gaze to me. "And internal affairs is going to be all over both of you like white on rice."

Hank inclines his head. "I know, sir."

I do the same. "I'll tell them whatever they need to know and cooperate with any investigations. But I can't offer you any names if I don't know them."

That should protect Reaper, Mouth, and Chaos from any criminal prosecution, assuming there isn't additional evidence somewhere that can be tied to them. But I'm not even worried about that.

They're true professionals who know what they're doing. After Chaos and Mouth took care of the few remaining men elsewhere in the facility, they did a full sweep to ensure nothing was left behind before they came to locate us. If there was anything to find, they would've found it and ensured it was taken care of. I have zero doubts about that. Which means they should be in the clear.

Hank, on the other hand...

He still sits, shoulders back, head held high despite the fact that he's tanking his career. And he's doing it for *me*.

I can barely find the words, but the captain stares at me, waiting for me to say something. "I'll take whatever punishment IA deems necessary for what I've done."

He shakes his head and scowls. "You could lose your badge over this, Viktoria." Another heavy sigh slips from his lips. "And I would ask you if it's worth it, but I've seen those girls. I heard about the conditions they were living in and what those fucking Russians intended to do with them. So, I know it was worth it. As angry as I am about the entire situation, I can't fully fault you for what you did." He turns his attention to Hank. "Now, Hank, I'm sorry to have to do this."

"I know, sir." Hanks reaches for his waistband and sets his badge and gun on the desk.

Is this really happening?

"Viktoria?" The captain raises an eyebrow at me. "I'm going to need yours, too. At least until IA finishes their investigation and determines if any further action is required."

I incline my head. "I understand."

Pulling out my badge and gun that I stopped at my place to grab on the way over here feels surreal, and my hand shakes so violently, it's almost embarrassing.

The captain nods to both of us. "Expect to hear from them soon."

I push up from my chair and follow Hank from the room in a trance, the last few minutes playing through my head like a bad horror movie. The moment we're far enough down the hall, I grab his forearm. He turns to face me, and I release my hold on him and scan the hallway to ensure we're alone.

"Are you insane? Why did you do that? Why would you—"

He steps up to me and embraces me in a very un-Hank-like hug. "I did it because you don't deserve to go down for any of this. I, on the other hand, knew the risk going in. I accepted it. Made peace with it. I can get another job, Vik. What I can't do, is watch you lose everything you worked so hard for all because your partner got a wild hair and went fucking rogue."

"Jesus, Hank..." I shake my head and pull back from him. "I really wish you hadn't done that."

He smirks at me. "I know, Vik, but I had to. Just stick to the story, and you'll be fine. You might get a mark in your file, and I wouldn't rule out a temporary suspension, but they won't fire you. This city needs good cops more now than ever. You're one of the best."

"What the hell are you going to do?"

Hank glances over his shoulder down the hallway and offers a shrug. "Maybe I'll join a motorcycle club." He tosses me a wink. "Right now, I'm going to go check on Anastasia and the kids to make sure they're settling in."

"You really like her."

He shrugs again, his eyes darting around the hallway, purposely avoiding mine. "It's complicated."

I snort. "You totally like her." I shake my head and sigh, "It can't be any more complicated than things are between me and Reaper."

He smirks. "Yeah, I bet. The two of you are like oil and vinegar. So, what's the deal? Is he planning on sticking around?"

"I wish I knew."

Fuck, I really wish I knew.

REAPER

I shuffle out of the bedroom, scrubbing my hand over my face, and find Chaos and Mouth sitting at the counter with what looks like might actually be edible pasta half-eaten in bowls in front of them.

"Hey, man." Chaos turns toward me on his stool and leans back against the counter. "Good to see you up. How you feeling?"

Mouth inclines his head toward me, then returns to his food.

I offer Chaos an annoyed look and heave myself onto the stool next to him with a grunt.

"That good, huh?"

"Fuck you, man. When was the last time you were shot?"

He rubs his jaw and pretends to think about it even though all three of us know exactly when it was. "Twelve months ago."

"Maybe you're due."

He shakes his head and chuckles. "I'd like to keep myself bullet-free for the foreseeable future."

"Wouldn't we all?"

Mouth snorts and nods, polishing off his meal.

Chaos opens his mouth, likely with another smartass remark, but we all freeze at the whine and rumble of the garage door downstairs going up. "Sounds like your woman's back."

I scowl at him. "She's not my woman."

He pops a piece of bread in his mouth and chews. "Sure seems like she is." With a shrug, he shoves away from the counter and motions for Mouth to follow him. "Going to grab a smoke out on the fire escape. Catch you later."

They climb through the open window onto the back fire escape, and I sigh and run a hand over my face while the elevator makes its way up with one very big complication inside.

I didn't know what to say when she left earlier. How to tell her that I might not be here when she got back. And honestly, if it weren't for my arm in a sling and a hole in my shoulder, all three of us would probably be long gone by now.

Watching her stand at that door with her back to me felt like waiting for a piece of myself to walk away, but I just couldn't get out the words I wanted to say. Not when I don't know what she wants. Not when our lives are so completely different. When *we're* so different.

The elevator reaches the loft, and Viktoria pulls open the metal gate and steps out. Her eyes lock with mine as she slowly makes her way across the room and settles on the stool next to me, her dark hair flowing around her so soft it makes my fingers itch to touch it.

"Where are Mouth and Chaos?"

I incline my head toward the fire escape. "Having a smoke."

She nods and blows out a long, slow breath like she's releasing all the stress of her day. That suggests her meeting did not go as planned.

I'm almost afraid to ask. "How did your meeting go?"

"About as well as can be expected. Especially because Hank threw himself on the proverbial sword and took the fall for everything."

"What?"

She nods, the exhaustion of the last few days creating dark bags around her eyes. "He told our captain that this was all him. That he called me with the location of the girls because he knew I was in the area and wanted them secured while he arrested Yankovich so that nobody would harm them."

"He arrested Yankovich?"

"Yep." She pops the *P* and leans forward, resting her elbows on the counter and shoving her hands back through her hair. "Surprised the hell out of me, too."

"So, you're getting at least half of what you wanted. He'll go to trial."

She shrugs. "Maybe. We'll see." Her gaze darts to me and softens slightly. "How are you feeling?"

I offer a little shrug, then wince and instantly regret it. "Pretty good."

Lightly drumming her nails on the counter, Vik swallows thickly and casts a glance in the direction the boys went. "When are you guys taking off?"

I sigh and run my hand through my hair, turning on the stool to face her. "I don't know. What's going to happen to you?"

She squeezes shut her eyes and releases a frustrated groan. "IA will be up my ass. I'm supposed to meet with them tomorrow, and then..." One of her shoulders rises and falls, and she finally opens her eyes to peer at me with a look that forms an ache in the center of my chest. "I don't know."

"Is there a chance you might keep your badge?"

"I hope so."

I clear my throat. "And...if not?"

She releases a long, heavy sigh and runs her hands through her hair, tugging at it gently. "I don't fucking know, Reaper. I feel like I don't know anything anymore. The last few weeks have been nothing but one mind-fuck after another."

"Is that what I am? A mind-fuck?"

Where the hell did that question come from? And why the hell do I sound so defensive?

It doesn't matter. It's hanging out there between us now, thickening the air with tension I could cut with the knife I keep in my boot.

She freezes and turns to face me, throwing up her hands —but whether in anger or frustration...it's impossible to tell. "I don't know *what* you are, Reaper."

"Yes, you do. You said it yourself...I'm a heartless killer."

"You're not heartless." She shakes her head and leans to brush her fingertips along my cheek and her thumb over my lips. "You try to hide it, but I can still see it in there under all those scars you don't want me to touch or tell me about."

Fuck...

There comes that damn tightening in my chest again, and I pull away from her touch, averting my gaze from her toward the window to the fire escape—where I would much rather be enjoying a smoke than having this conversation.

"You don't want to hear about that, Vik. You don't want to hear my horror stories."

"I wouldn't ask if I didn't want to."

"What happened last night at that warehouse..." I glance at her and tighten my fist on the counter. "It's nothing compared to some of the things I've seen, some of the things I've done."

The reasons for the scars and the drinking that eventually got me discharged. The reason I never go home to see Mom and Dad—that I can't look them in the eye, knowing what I've done and continue to do.

Vik slides from her stool and nudges my legs open until I turn to fully face her again and let her step between them. She captures my face in her palms and tilts it up toward her. "I don't know if I'm going to be a cop anymore or not. What I do know...is I want to know *you*. I want to know Roderick Dixon. *And*...I want to know Reaper. I want to know what turned you *into* Reaper. Why you'd rather be him than Roderick. I want to know everything you're willing to tell me. Everything that's happened in your life is what brought you to me, to this moment in time. One I don't want to let slip past us."

Her words cut me deeper than any knife ever has. It's the thing that I've always secretly longed to hear but have always been terrified of at the same time. "That's what you want? For me to stay?"

"Or go..." The corner of her mouth twitches up. "And I'll come with you."

"You would leave? Just like that?"

"I don't even know if I'll have my badge anymore, at least here in New York."

If it were only that easy, riding off into the sunset

together. "What about what I do, Viktoria? You told me there is no place in this world for vigilantes who act outside the law."

She offers a little halfhearted shrug. "I may have taken a hard line on that when we first met, but after what's happened with Yankovich, I think vigilantism could have its place. And I also don't think what we did over the course of the last few weeks is what you're doing every day."

Pretty bold assumption on her part.

We haven't exactly discussed what I was doing prior to appearing in New York, aside from my little mission in Manila that brought me to The Big Apple.

I swallow thickly. "I haven't been doing much since I was discharged. Some favors for some friends, and that's about it."

She can make her own assumptions about the types of "favors" I've been doing, and something tells me that by now, she won't be far off from the truth.

One of her hands slides from my cheek, down my neck, to press against my chest. "And will you continue to do it? Favors for friends?"

If I told her *no,* I would be lying. And I don't want to make promises I can't keep.

"I've been thinking about setting up a business. Private security firm with Chaos and Mouth and maybe a few other guys who are about to get out. We would likely still do some work and *favors* for people, but a legitimate security firm would bring in a nice stream of income."

A grin plays on her perfect lips. "That sounds perfect for you."

"It might be." I suck in a deep breath, building up my nerve to say these final words to her. Words I never imagined saying to anyone before. "It would be perfect if you're by my side."

Her hand freezes on my cheek, green eyes sparkling with unshed tears. "Is that really what you want?"

It's the same question I've asked myself a thousand times since I first kissed her. The one that has rattled around my head so much that it left permanent marks. But after so long not knowing the answer, now, it seems so obvious.

"All I know is I want you, Viktoria. I want your smart-ass mouth, your attitude. I want you to challenge me and fight with me so that we can make up the way we have been. I want to be able to sleep at night, and the only time that's ever happened is with you. That's what I want. If you do, too."

She doesn't answer me, just leans in and presses her lips to mine in a kiss so sweet that it's almost sickening. But instead of rejecting it, rejecting her and protecting myself like I always have for my entire adult life, I wrap my good arm around her and pull her up against me, ignoring the bite of pain it causes as I devour her mouth and deepen our kiss.

I knew a reckoning was coming, that someone would have to pay for what they had done to Eva, to *all* those girls. I just never imagined I would be coming out feeling more alive than I ever have been and with the woman who could have ruined the entire mission.

The woman who now holds my heart and my future.

———

Want more from the Sins of the Mafia World?

Grab the Sins of the Mafia Collections here: https://
books2read.com/rl/SinsoftheMafiaWorld

Also, don't miss Hank and Anastasia's story, *Dead or Alive*,
written by Janine Infante Bosco which is available now!

Sign up for Gwyn's newsletter to stay up to date on releases
and other news: www.gwynmcnamee.com/newsletter

ABOUT THE AUTHOR

Gwyn McNamee is an attorney, writer, wife, and mother (to one human baby and two fur babies). Originally from the Midwest, Gwyn relocated to her husband's home town of Las Vegas in 2015 and is enjoying her respite from the cold and snow. Gwyn has been writing down her crazy stories and ideas for years and finally decided to share them with the world. She loves to write stories with a bit of suspense and action mingled with romance and heat.

When she isn't either writing or voraciously devouring any books she can get her hands on, Gwyn is busy adding to her tattoo collection, golfing, and stirring up trouble with her perfect mix of sweetness and sarcasm (usually while wearing heels).

Gwyn loves to hear from her readers. Here is where you can find her:

Website:
https://www.gwynmcnamee.com
Newsletter:
www.gwynmcnamee.com/newsletter
Facebook:
https://www.facebook.com/AuthorGwynMcNamee/
Twitter:
https://twitter.com/GwynMcNamee
Instagram:

https://www.instagram.com/gwynmcnamee
Bookbub:
https://www.bookbub.com/authors/gwyn-mcnamee
FB Reader Group:
https://www.facebook.com/groups/1667380963540655/